A WITCH FOR MR. HOLIDAY

WITCHES OF CHRISTMAS GROVE, BOOK 1

DEANNA CHASE

ABOUT THIS BOOK

Welcome to Christmas Grove, where holiday magic and matchmaking are in the air.

When Rex Holiday walks into the charming town of Christmas Grove, all he plans to do is to spend the season helping out at his buddy's Christmas tree farm. What he doesn't expect is for an overzealous matchmaker to slip a love potion into his cider. But the joke's on the resident matchmaker, because not even a potent love spell can break through the walls he's built around his heart. But when the girl next door catches his eye, some of his barriers start to crumble. Still, Rex Holiday's time in Christmas Grove is only temporary. He can't afford to fall in love. Or can he?

Holly Reineer is a powerful spirit witch who can see the future for everyone. Everyone but herself that is. And when Rex Holiday walks into her life, she sees his, too. He's destined for a big corporate job all the way across the country. So when he starts to show interest in her, she knows it's only temporary, and Holly's not interested in a fling. She wants her happily-ever-after. But he's very hard to resist... Can a love spell rewrite the future? If so, Holly will need to learn to follow her heart and, for once, trust what she can't see.

CHAPTER 1

*S*pecial Delivery for Holly Reineer.

Holly stared at the elegantly wrapped package and frowned. The late November sun glinted off the shiny silver paper, making her squint from the reflection as she tried to rack her brain for who might have sent her the present.

It most likely was from someone in town. Lemon from the Christmas Grove Express had delivered it herself. Which meant either someone had sent Lemon the package to wrap and deliver, or someone had wrapped it themselves and hired her to deliver it. Holly knew the latter scenario was most likely. Lemon was notoriously bad in the wrapping department. If left to her, she'd shove the gift in a bag, throw some tissue paper on top, and call it a day.

"What do you have there? Looks like Santa came early this year." Ilsa McKenzie, Holly's best friend, strolled up onto the porch of Holly's yellow Victorian. "Who's it from?"

Holly shrugged and sat in her porch swing. "No idea. It was just delivered."

Ilsa twisted her long black hair up into a messy bun and sat next to her friend, eyeing the package. "Well. Aren't you going to open it?"

"I was thinking of putting it under the tree so I'll have something to open on Christmas morning." Holly's parents had passed in a freak accident eighteen years before, and since she didn't have any siblings, holidays were a little light on the presents. Ilsa always got her something, but they had a tradition of trading gifts on Christmas Eve every year.

"No way! What if it's a puppy? You can't leave it in there for a month." Ilsa grabbed the package and shook it gently.

Holly rolled her eyes. "It's not a puppy. You just have no patience."

"True." Ilsa winked at her friend. "My impulse control is non-existent. Speaking of impulse control, did you see the new guy in town? He's gorgeous. I might have accidentally-on-purpose grabbed his ass in the grocery store this morning."

"You mean Rex Holiday?" Holly asked, trying to ignore the sick jealous feeling in her stomach. "Did you... um..."

"Ask him out?" she asked, her eyebrows raised and a challenging glint in her eye.

Holly narrowed her eyes at her friend. "You know, don't you?"

Ilsa threw her head back and laughed. "Who doesn't know? That love spell is the talk of the town."

Two days earlier, at the Christmas tree lighting in Christmas Grove's town square, Rex Holiday had unwittingly hit Holly with a love spell. Now he was all she could think about. The tall guy with sun bleached light brown hair and bright blue eyes made her want to throw herself at him. It wasn't just his classic good looks. He had an easy smile and a confidence about him that drew her in and made butterflies flutter in her stomach that she knew had nothing to do with the spell. Or at least they hadn't when she'd met him in Love Potions, the town's chocolate shop, ten minutes before the love spell incident.

"I swear, if I didn't love Mrs. Pottson so much, I'd hex that old witch myself," Holly said.

Ilsa laughed harder.

"Shush." Holly scowled at her friend. "It isn't funny. He's leaving. Like they all do. What am I supposed to do? Date him? Really? What if I fall for him like I did Ryan a few years ago? Remember what happened that time? I spent an entire weekend in bed, crying my eyes out and eating two pounds of chocolate by myself. If you hadn't cut me off, I'd probably weigh more than the house by now."

"Ryan was different," Ilsa said, waving a hand. "You didn't know going in that he was going to leave. But Rex Holiday? He's here for a month. And he's hot as sin." She fanned a hand in front of her face. "What's wrong with a little fling? A girl needs a little affection every now and then, right? Let your hair down. Have a little holiday romance. You deserve it."

Holly fiddled with the bow of the package. She'd love to throw caution to the wind and date Rex for the next month. On an intellectual level, she knew her friend was right. Holly should enjoy herself. She was thirty-two years old and had only really dated two people. One she'd known would leave, but she'd believed him when he said he'd come back no matter what. The other one? He had come back, only to leave again. She'd learned the hard way to trust her visions. They never lied.

"Come on, Hols. You need a date to the Christmas ball anyway. We both know there isn't anyone else in town you want to go with," Ilsa coaxed.

"That's still a few weeks away." Holly rose from the swing

and headed inside with Ilsa right behind her. After she placed the present under her ten-foot Christmas tree that filled the front window, she turned to her friend. "Ready for some hot chocolate?"

"You're trying to change the subject." Ilsa glanced at the present. "I bet it's from Rex."

Holly sighed. "Ilsa, why would you think that? I've only talked to the guy for a total of maybe five minutes. He's not buying me gifts."

"Who else would it be from?" Ilsa followed Holly into the large kitchen at the back of the house and glanced out the window toward the Christmas tree farm next door. "It's not from me. And you haven't heard from Ryan in two years."

Holly flinched. Ryan was still a sore spot even though she was completely over him. It was just hard to move on from the damage he'd caused.

"Sorry," Ilsa whispered. "I didn't mean to bring him up."

"Maybe it's a secret Santa gift," Holly mused. "We do that at the library, you know."

"Sure, Hols." Ilsa gave her arm a squeeze and slid into one of the chairs at the breakfast table. She rested her chin in her hand and stared dreamily through half-lidded eyes. "Can I tell you about Zach now?"

"My neighbor Zach?" Holly asked.

"Yeah. That one." Ilsa's lips curved into a small smile. "We had a moment yesterday."

"What kind of moment? The kind where you flirted with him and he ran away? Or the kind where he flirted with you and you pinched his ass?" Ilsa was a lot of things, but subtle wasn't one of them.

She laughed. "Both of those do sound like me, don't they?"

Holly nodded and went to work on fixing them both some

real hot chocolate, the kind made with milk and actual chocolate bars, not powder. She poured milk into the pan and dropped in the chocolate, but before she could get her wooden spoon, her vision blurred slightly, and when she refocused, she let out a small gasp.

"What did you see?" Ilsa asked immediately, her voice full of excitement.

"Oh, dammit, Ilsa." She spun around, her face pinched in frustration. "You committed me to a double date?"

Her friend just shrugged and batted her eyelashes at her as she asked, "Are we having fun?"

Holly moaned her disapproval. In her vision, she saw herself and Ilsa playing mini golf with Rex and Zach. Ilsa was in Zach's arms, while Holly was lying on the putting green, laid out flat and dying of embarrassment. Rex was peering down at her, his brow wrinkled with concern. "You are. I'm an idiot."

"Oh, good." Ilsa clapped her hands together, and Holly glared at her again. "Oops. I just meant that means I'm successful in getting you to go. It's tomorrow night. Six o'clock. We're having dinner and then heading to Karma Arcade. They're hosting couples' night, no kids." She smiled brightly at Holly and slid out of her chair. "I better go while I'm ahead. See you tomorrow!"

"Forget it!" Holly called after her. "I'm not going. I don't care what my vision says."

"Six o'clock. Wear the green dress. It shows off your eyes," Ilsa called back just before Holly heard her front door open and then slam closed.

"Traitor," Holly mumbled and turned off the burner for the hot chocolate. She was no longer in the mood. Instead, she brewed herself a cup of coffee and went out on the back porch to watch the sun set over the foothills.

Holly loved her little slice of heaven. Ten years ago, when her grandmother passed, she inherited the Victorian and the twenty acres it sat on. She utilized a couple of acres for her berry farm and leased the rest to Zach Frost for his Christmas Tree farm next door. It worked for her. What else was she going to do with twenty acres of land by herself? Besides, she loved the Frost family. She'd grown up with Zach and loved him like a brother.

"Spruce!" a man's faint voice sounded from the trees.

Damn. What was that dog getting into now? Zach had gotten a Lab puppy about five months earlier, and the thing was always getting into something. Holly stood and scanned the small clearing for the rambunctious dog.

The man called for the pup again, but his voice sounded even farther away, as if he'd turned around. She was about to sit back down when the golden dog darted out from between the trees carrying a bright-white stuffed animal in his mouth as he ran full speed across the yard.

"Spruce! Stop!" Holly cried and jumped down into her damp yard. It had rained the night before, leaving her lawn soggy.

The dog didn't even look Holly's way as he kept running straight for the opening to the berry farm.

"No!" Holly said again and snapped her fingers.

The dog suddenly paused, and it was at that moment that the stuffed animal in Spruce's mouth twitched.

Holly's eyes widened as she realized the animal wasn't stuffed at all. It was a real live bunny that Spruce had between his jaws. "Drop the bunny," Holly ordered, quickly moving toward the dog.

Spruce just stood there, his head tilted, jaws unmoving as

he looked at Holly, as if he had no idea what Holly wanted him to do.

"Listen, pup," Holly said when she got within a few feet of him. "I realize you think Cottontail there is a toy, but you could be hurting her. You need to let her go."

The dog didn't move a muscle.

"Come on, sweetie. We all know you aren't a killer." Holly slowly reached a hand out, placing her palm right under Spruce's muzzle. She was right there to catch the poor frightened animal the minute Spruce released it. "Drop the bunny," Holly ordered in a quiet but commanding tone.

Spruce's eyes narrowed slightly, and Holly held her breath, terrified the dog was going to bolt.

"You're okay, Spruce. We've got this," Holly soothed. "Let Auntie Holly have the bunny." She reached up to scratch the dog's ear, something she knew the pup was a sucker for. And after a few moments, Spruce's jaw relaxed, and the bunny fell out of his grip and right into Holly's other hand. But the bunny was too big for her to hold onto and flopped to the ground at her feet.

Holly let out a gasp when the poor thing didn't move, and she bent to retrieve the creature. But before she could scoop the bunny up, a loud branch snapped just beyond the tree line and Spruce bolted again, this time running right into Holly and knocking her flat on her back. As the dog scrambled by her, mud and clumps of grass splattered all over her as the wetness of the yard seeped through her jeans and long-sleeved T-shirt.

"Holly?" a man said as a shadow fell over her.

She wiped a drop of mud off her eyelid and blinked up at the man. Late afternoon sunlight glowed around him, causing his face to be hidden in shadow. But she could tell he was holding the bunny to his chest, stroking its long ears. "Is the bunny okay?"

"Looks like it," the man said. "Are you?"

"I'm fine." She planted both hands and tried to push herself up. But the grass was too slick and her right hand slid out from under her, causing her to slam right back down onto the ground. And this time when she looked up at the man, he'd shifted just enough that there was no mistaking him. The man who'd just watched her flail in an impromptu mud bath was none other than Rex Holiday.

CHAPTER 2

*C*oncern mixed with amusement as Rex peered down at Holly Reineer. To say he was happy to run into her was an understatement. He'd thought of almost nobody else since he'd met the pretty redhead at the chocolate store. But he wouldn't have chosen for Zach's dog to run her down and send her flailing. She was flat on her back with mud speckling her gorgeous heart-shaped face, and she had a frown on her lips. "Are you okay?"

"Sure, I just need to get up."

Rex extended a hand to her. "I can help with that."

"I've got this," she said, scrambling to get her feet under her. But as soon as she put weight on her left foot, she let out a yelp of pain and slid back down into the mud.

"You're hurt," Rex said, crouching down beside her. He needed to get her inside and warm her up before the cold chilled her to the bone. Not to mention her foot needed attention. Luckily, he was just the man to help. "Here. Take the bunny."

She shook her head and opened her mouth to say

something, but Rex put the animal in her hands and cut her off.

"I'll get you inside, but I need my hands free." Without waiting for her inevitable protest, Rex quickly scooped the woman up in his arms and carried her and the bunny into the back of her house. Bypassing the large kitchen, he moved around to the breakfast table and gently placed her in one of the wooden chairs. After carefully propping her foot on another chair, he asked, "Where can I find your hand towels?"

Holly blinked at him, still clutching the bunny.

"Hey," he said, placing a light palm on her cheek. Her eyes were wide and her face too pale. He didn't know if she was in shock from her injury or because he'd taken charge without consulting her. Either way, everything inside of him demanded that he soothe her. "You're okay. I'm just going to get a towel so I can clean you up a bit."

"Right," she whispered and cut her gaze to the kitchen. "They're next to the sink. Top drawer."

"Got it." Rex hurried into the kitchen, grabbed a bag of frozen berries from the freezer, and found two towels. After wetting one, he quickly returned to Holly's side.

Her head was tilted back, and she was muttering something about being a klutzy idiot.

"Nah. You're a hero. You saved the bunny." He smiled down at her, amused at her annoyance.

"I broke my foot." She scowled as she glanced at her swelling ankle.

He instantly felt like an ass for not paying more attention to her injury. "Here. Let me see what I can do." Rex knelt near her foot and carefully untied her tennis shoe. "How much does it hurt?"

"Enough that I can't walk on it."

"Right." He nodded. "I saw that. Can you give it to me on a scale of one to ten, with one being doesn't hurt at all and ten meaning you're ready to pass out?"

She closed her eyes and clutched the bunny to her as she said, "Eight? Seven? I don't know. It's starting to throb."

Something inside of him twisted. He hated seeing her suffering. Rex placed a soft hand over one of hers. "I can help. Do you trust me?"

Holly kept her eyes closed tight as she whispered, "Yes."

He let out a breath and couldn't say exactly why her answer meant so much to him. He supposed it was the love spell that Mrs. Pottson had slipped into his cider, but he couldn't shake the feeling that this was more than that. Like he *needed* someone to need him. Son of a... What was wrong with him? He'd just met this woman. Why did he want to pack her up, take her back to his cabin, and tuck her into his bed where he could keep an eye on her? He shook his head as if to dislodge the unfamiliar emotions and gently removed her shoe and sock from her injured foot. "Is this okay, Holly?"

"Yes," she whispered.

"Good. I'm going to put this bag of frozen berries on your ankle and then throw together a salve that will help with the swelling. Do you have a pain potion in the house?"

Holly opened her eyes and met his gaze. "I don't think so."

"Okay. Hold tight. I can pull something together." He ran gentle fingers over her swelling ankle and released the tiniest bit of his magic.

A small sigh escaped Holly's lips, and the tension lining her face eased. "Oh, my goodness," she said. "How did you do that?"

He used the wet towel to wipe the mud off her face and smiled self-consciously as he said, "It's a trick I learned from my grandmother. But don't get too excited. It's just temporary.

Let me get the potion and salve made. They should help until we can get you to a healer."

"Okay." She turned her attention to the bunny and stroked its ears as it snuggled in closer to her. And when a tiny smile claimed her lips, the ache in his own chest disappeared knowing he'd helped ease her suffering.

Rex made himself at home in her kitchen, raiding her extensive herb cabinet and, to his relief, her well-stocked root storage. After whipping up a basic pain potion, he pulled out the ginger root, cayenne pepper, and coconut oil. Once he ground it all together with a mortar and pestle, he dipped his fingers into the salve and imagined Holly's ankle completely healed. Magic sparked into the concoction, making it glow. He took a moment to mix the salve and by the time he removed his fingers, he was left with a vibrant sunset-orange ointment.

"Holly, are you and the bunny doing okay?"

"The bunny is fine. She's sleeping," she said. "But my ankle is starting to throb again."

"I've got you covered." Rex moved back over to the breakfast table and handed her the pain potion. "Drink that before I work on your ankle."

Rex waited until Holly gulped down all of the potion. When he heard her let out a sigh of relief as the painkiller started to do its job, he removed the frozen berries from her ankle and gently rubbed in the salve over the swelling.

"What the heck is that?" Holly asked, her eyes wide with surprise as she wiggled her toes. "It tingles and feels... good."

"Just a little earth magic salve." He pulled out a chair and sat next to her. "So, what are you going to name that bunny?"

Holly glanced down at the sleeping animal. "What makes you think I'm keeping her?"

Rex didn't miss the fact that her eyes had started to sparkle and the color had returned to her cheeks. His grandmother would be proud. He'd done his job well. "Because you've decided the bunny is a she and you're holding her like you're never going to let her go."

Chuckling, Holly nodded. "You're probably right. I was terrified when I saw Spruce had her. That dog. I swear."

"Dammit," Rex muttered, getting to his feet. "I forgot all about Spruce." He hurried to the back door. "I'll be right back so we can get you to a healer. Let me just make sure Spruce hasn't gotten into any more trouble."

"Oh, no. Don't worry about me. I can call Ilsa. She'll get me to the healer," Holly insisted.

Rex shook his head. "Don't even think about it. I want to explain to the healer what I did so she gets the full picture."

"I—"

"I'll be right back." Rex strode out the door and nearly tripped over Spruce, who was lying on the porch pretending to be innocent. He let out a snort of irritation. "Really?"

Spruce lifted his head and gave him the saddest puppy dog eyes he'd ever seen.

"Jeez, boy. Don't go looking for sympathy from me." He pulled a leash from his pocket and hooked it to his collar. "Let's get you home."

Five minutes later, Rex returned to Holly's Victorian only to find her and the bunny missing. "Holly?" he called out, moving into her front sitting room. No answer. Torn between invading her privacy and making sure she was okay, he stood at the bottom of her stairs and contemplated searching the house.

"Damn," he muttered and ran up the stairs. When he didn't find her on the second floor, he spied another set of stairs and ended up in a third-floor, bird's-eye sunroom. Three half-finished landscape paintings lined one wall and right in the middle there was an easel with a large canvas. He moved around to check out her current work in progress and sucked in a sharp breath.

There was no missing the familiar angular jaw and slightly crooked nose. Holly Reineer was painting a portrait of him.

CHAPTER 3

*H*olly was simply mortified. Leave it to her to find herself splattered in the mud with a sprained ankle in front of the one man she couldn't stop thinking about. Sure, she'd been hit with a love spell. But there was a truth she hadn't been willing to admit to herself. It started the first day Rex Holiday had rolled into town and Holly spotted him from her third-floor studio. It wasn't long before she'd started sketching him. How could she resist? There was a magnetism that drew her to him. Some sort of inner spark that she couldn't help but be drawn to. She was lying to herself when she said she wasn't interested.

Man, was she interested. Holly had first seen him a few weeks earlier as he walked the perimeter of the Christmas tree farm with Zach. The pull she'd felt that day had hit her hard and settled deep in her bones. She'd almost run out of her house to introduce herself, but then the vision of him living his life in New York flashed in her mind and all the excitement fled, leaving her deflated.

She hadn't felt anything like it since the day Ryan had

walked into her life three years ago. And the memory of what it felt like when Ryan left was still too raw for her to consider letting anyone else into her life that she knew was leaving. It was just too hard. Still, even though she knew Rex would be gone sometime before mid-January and the possibility of a relationship with him was impossible, she still cared that she'd made a complete fool of herself. Why couldn't she be the cool mysterious girl for once instead of the nerdy librarian?

She pulled her car into a space right in front of Healer Harrison's office and glanced in the rearview mirror. Grimacing, she ran her hand through her mud-caked hair and wished the world would just swallow her whole. At least she hadn't let Rex drive her to town while she looked like a victim from *The Walking Dead*.

Talk about embarrassing.

Guh. Holly took a peek in the oversized pocket of her sweater, checking on the bunny. The little animal was curled up, her eyes closed as she snoozed comfortably. "At least one of us is doing well."

Holly pushed her door open and swung her legs out of the car. This was where things were going to get tricky. She'd limped out of her house and into the car, but she couldn't actually feel her foot at the moment, which would make walking an issue. It took some maneuvering, but she did manage to awkwardly haul herself up on her right foot.

"Now what?" she asked no one as she glanced around, looking for someone to help her hobble inside.

"Holly?" Candy Price asked, poking her head out of the office door. "Do you need help?"

Holly let out a relieved breath. "Yes. I've hurt my foot and can't walk. Can someone help me inside?"

"Of course," the receptionist said. "Let me get a wheelchair.

Hang tight. I'll be right back." She disappeared back into the office, leaving Holly balancing on one foot while clutching her car door.

A red truck pulled into the space beside her, and much to Holly's dismay, Rex jumped out and ran over to her side. Frowning, he shook his head and said, "You were supposed to wait for me."

"I didn't want to bother you anymore," she said and inwardly cringed. What a copout. She'd known he was headed back to her house and bolted anyway. Well, more like hobbled, but she hadn't wasted any time.

He glanced down at her injured foot. "Let's get you inside. I need to speak to your healer."

"They're bringing a wheelchair," she said, glancing at the office as if she could will someone to appear. But no one did.

Rex ignored her comment, and without any preamble, swept her up into his arms.

"Wait!" Holly cried and reached for her pocket, making sure the bunny was safe. She pulled her out and cradled her to her chest with one hand while Rex carried Holly into the healer's office.

"Oh, good," Candy said, looking relieved. She tucked a strand of her dark curly hair behind one ear and hurried out from behind the desk to open the door to the patient area. "One wheelchair is in use and the other has a broken wheel. We've got someone working on it, but it was going to be a minute."

"Good thing I showed up," Rex said with a smile.

"I guess so," Holly muttered, wondering if she could devise a disappearing spell. Not likely. She was a spirit witch, meaning she often had visions but didn't have the magic to cast any useful spells. Seeing into the future wasn't exactly a picnic.

Why couldn't she have air magic that would help her clean her house or keep her dry when it started to rain? Nope. She had to deal in the metaphysical world.

"Right through here," Candy said, leading them into an exam room that looked more like the front parlor of an elegant Victorian. There was a red velvet couch against one wall and two matching armchairs sitting across from a wooden desk. The wood floors were a rich mahogany color that matched the wood-planked ceiling. The only part of the office that resembled a healer's exam room was the exam table off to the side that was made up with a fuzzy Christmas blanket. Holly wondered how they kept the room sterile.

"On the table?" Rex asked.

"Yes, please," Candy said. "Healer Harrison will be right with you."

Rex carefully lowered Holly to the exam table and pulled a small rolling stool over so he could sit next to her. "How does the foot feel?"

"Numb," she said and closed her eyes, trying not to think about the fact she was the damsel in distress who looked like she'd been mud wrestling.

"That's a good sign. Means it's healing," Rex said.

She heard him get up and walk across the office. It wasn't long before he was back, and she could feel him hovering over her. Without even opening her eyes and looking into his handsome face, her skin started to tingle. Dammit if she didn't want him to touch her.

"I found a pillow to put under your foot," he said.

"Okay."

Rex wrapped his strong hand around her shin and lifted. His fingers sent warm tingles up her leg, making a shiver spark over her skin. Her eyes flew open, and she found herself staring into the crystal blue eyes of the most handsome man to step into Christmas Grove in over a decade. Goddess above. Why did he have to be so good looking? Not that his looks were the only part of him that attracted her. There was that undeniable magnetism that drew her in. Hell, she hadn't even been looking at him, but then he touched her leg and the next thing she knew she was ready to throw herself at him... injured foot and all.

"Holly?" Healer Harrison said as the door opened. A tall blond woman swept into the room and strode to Holly's side. "Who's this little one?" she asked, eyeing the bunny.

"The creature I was trying to save when I went down." Holly stroked the ears of the sleeping animal.

"Holly's a hero," Rex said. "She saved the bunny from Zach's overzealous dog."

"I see." After a quick glance at Holly's ankle, the healer turned to Rex. "What happened?"

"I slipped," Holly said, not at all pleased the healer hadn't addressed her directly. Rhina Harrison was going to get an earful later when Rex wasn't there to be witness to her meltdown.

"I think it's a sprain, but I can't be sure," Rex said.

The healer ran her fingers over the now only slightly swollen ankle. She closed her eyes, appearing to assess the injury with her mind's eye. "Doesn't seem too bad. I'd suggest some pain potions and staying off of it for a few days."

"Is that all?" Holly asked, her eyebrows rising in surprise as she stared down at her foot. "It was the size of a softball before Rex put that salve on it."

Rhina's eyes popped open, and she turned to stare at Rex. "You put a magical salve on this?"

He nodded. "Ginger root, cayenne pepper, and coconut oil."

"Magic infused?" she asked.

"Yeah." He shoved his hands in his front pockets and rocked back on his heels.

"I see. This changes things then." The healer retreated to the cabinets behind her desk, pulled out her own salve, and then returned to Holly's side. She reached over and squeezed Rex's arm. "Nice job, by the way. I don't think I've ever seen a homemade salve work as well as yours did today."

Rex gave her a tiny half-shrug. "I just did what I could."

Healer Harrison let out a snort. "I bet if you wanted to get your healer's license you'd pass with flying colors."

"I'm usually better when I'm getting my hands dirty." Rex turned his attention to Holly and gave her a wink.

Fire! Red hot fire shot through Holly's body. If Rhina hadn't been in the room, Holly thought she might have grabbed Rex by the shirt and yanked him down to give him a searing kiss. Whoa. Holly wanted to fan herself. Never in her life had a man affected her like Rex Holiday.

"Uh, what?" Rhina asked him, laughing.

"I'm an earth witch," he told her. "I contract with farmers to help their crops."

"Ah, I see. That makes sense." Most healers specialized in earth magic, but not all. Still chuckling to herself, the healer took her time inspecting Holly's lower leg, ankle, and foot. After applying a salve of her own, her fingertips sparked with healer magic that wrapped around Holly's foot as if it were a bandage. "There. That should do it. I suspect you'll be as good as new by the end of the week." She turned to Rex. "I'm glad you told me what you did. I would've missed it otherwise."

"Holly," the healer said, turning her attention to her patient. "I'm prescribing a special potion to keep the inflammation from coming back. Take it twice a day for the next three days, okay?"

"Okay."

"Rex," she said, her eyes glinting as she turned to him. "I'd love to talk to you more about what you did here. Maybe we can get dinner sometime? I've been dying to try that new restaurant, Mistletoe's. There's supposed to be live music tomorrow night on the square. We could make a night of it."

What the hell? Was Rhina Harrison actually asking her guy out right in front of her? Before Rex could respond, Holly blurted, "Sorry, Rhina. Rex and I already have plans tomorrow night."

"Oh." Rhina glanced between Holly and Rex and then frowned as realization dawned in her eyes. "I see."

Rex raised one eyebrow at Holly as if to say, *Oh, really?*

"Zach and Ilsa are expecting us," Holly told him.

His lips twitched into a tiny smile as he nodded. "Right. Mini golf was it?"

The healer cleared her throat. "You need to stay off that foot for a few days, otherwise, you could reinjure it."

"No problem." Rex gave her a solemn nod. "I'll make sure she doesn't aggravate it. We'll have coffee and cheesecake while the other two compete for the mini golf championship." He turned his attention to Holly. "Ready?"

"Yep." She started to swing her legs off the exam table, but Rex placed a hand on her shoulder, stopping her.

"No need to wait for that wheelchair. I've got you," he said.

And this time when Rex swept her up in his arms, she was ready for it, pleased even to be pressed against his chest. Still clutching the sleeping bunny, she called over his shoulder to Rhina. "Thanks for the help."

"Anytime," Rhina said with a sigh. As they headed down the

hallway, Holly was certain she heard the other woman mumble, "Always a day late and a dollar short."

"She should have tried a love potion," Holly muttered back.

Rex let out a bark of laughter and smiled down at her. "Lucky for me, I saw you first."

"What? You're not interested in Rhina? She's sophisticated. Pretty too."

"Nope. I prefer stubborn redheads," he said.

"Love potions do that to people, Rex."

He shook his head, amusement dancing in his blue eyes. "Perhaps. But I knew when I met you at Love Potions I wanted to take you out, so let's not pretend the love spell is the only reason I'm interested."

Her mouth went dry as she realized what she'd done. She'd just claimed him in front of the town healer and had agreed to the double date she'd told Ilsa she had no intention of going on. And now, because of her ankle, their date had turned into dessert and coffee, which for some reason seemed a heck of a lot more like a real date than a foursome at the town arcade.

"Are you okay, Holly?" he asked as they stopped at the receptionist's desk.

"Yeah, sure. Why?"

He gently set her down so she could balance on her good foot. "You just seem a little…"

"Annoyed? Irritated? Impatient?" she supplied.

"No. I don't think that's it." He tilted his head to the side to study her. "More like nervous."

Sweat prickled at the back of her neck, because dammit, he was right.

CHAPTER 4

"*I*'m not nervous," Holly insisted as she handed her credit card over to the receptionist so she could settle her bill. "I was just wondering how I'm going to work off those extra calories if you insist on cheesecake while our friends putter around the miniature golf course."

Sure she wasn't. He might've believed her if she hadn't kept chewing on her lower lip. But he wasn't going to call her out again. Instead, he grinned and said, "I have a few ideas."

Her face flushed bright red, and he wondered if he could tease that blush out of the rest of her body. It was a fantasy he'd already decided he needed to forget. Because when she'd called him temporary, no truer words had ever been spoken. Rex was scheduled to fly out to New York just as soon as the holidays were over, where he'd start his new job with a corporate organic farming organization. The job would send him all over the country where he'd oversee the agricultural health of the farms they owned.

"Stop flirting with me," she said, but there wasn't any conviction in her tone. "Let's just be... friends."

"Friends," he said, nodding his agreement. Sure. He could do that. Right? "Works for me. Does that mean you would let your new friend cook dinner for you? Someone needs to feed you. It might as well be me."

The receptionist handed back Holly's card along with a receipt and told them to have a good evening. As Rex maneuvered Holly out of the office, she said, "I can call—"

"Ilsa?" he asked with one raised eyebrow.

"Right. She'll bring me soup or something."

Rex grinned. "Nope. I overheard her telling Zach she was headed to Sacramento for the night. Something about seeing her niece's ballet recital."

"Oh, crap. That's right." She blew out a breath, sending a lock of her hair flying. "Well, I can just order some pasta from Pine Needles and have Christmas Grove Express pick it up for me. There's no need for you to keep being inconvenienced by me."

"I'm not inconvenienced." He let her down when they arrived at the passenger side of her car and said, "I'll drive you home in your car. Zach will bring me back for my truck." He fully expected her to balk at his offer, but to his surprise, she gave him a grateful smile, opened the door, and slid into the seat.

"Thanks," she said after he was situated behind the wheel.

"Don't mention it. This is what friends do. Or so I hear."

She laughed, handed him the keys, and once again cuddled the bunny as she said, "It is indeed. Now take me home so I can get into the shower while my new friend makes me something fabulous for dinner."

"You don't have to ask me twice," he said, trying to ignore the implications of the flutter in his chest. *Friends*, he told himself. *Just friends.* But when he looked over at her and took

24

in the way her red hair framed her face and the sweet smile on her lips as she gazed down at the bunny, he knew he'd never think of her as just a *friend*.

IT TOOK everything Rex had to leave Holly in her bathroom alone with the shower running. After they returned to her Victorian, she asked him to retrieve a set of crutches she had in the hall closet, and then he'd watched her struggle to make it halfway up the stairs before he was able to convince her to let him carry her the rest of the way. She hadn't exactly been thrilled about it, but practicality had won out, and she relented.

Now he could hear the shower running, and it was killing him. His body was warring with his mind. The thought of her under the warm spray, slicked with soap, made him imagine all kinds of things he shouldn't be thinking about a friend. And then there was the very real possibility that she might lose her balance. Suddenly, he wished Ilsa hadn't been out of town so that she could help Holly. Even if it meant he was no longer needed for dinner duty.

While Holly cleaned up, Rex took care of the bunny by finding a cardboard box, a blanket, some lettuce, and a water dish. He placed the box on the floor in the corner of the kitchen where he could keep an eye on her. It wasn't long before the rabbit found the lettuce and water. Once she had her fill, she curled up in the corner, content to snooze the rest of the evening away.

Then he got to work on raiding Holly's kitchen for dinner ideas. He was delighted to find the refrigerator and cabinets stocked. It meant he didn't need to run out to find ingredients.

In fact, the kitchen had just about everything an amateur chef might need. In no time, he had a mushroom risotto cooking while he pan-fried some chicken. He was just turning the burners off and getting ready to plate their dinner when he heard Holly clear her throat.

He turned to find her leaning against the doorframe that led from the kitchen to the front living room. Her still wet hair had been pulled up into a messy bun, and she was wearing yoga pants that hugged every curve and a form-fitting t-shirt. She was rosy pink from the shower and looked like every teenager's girl-next-door fantasy. "You were supposed to text me when you were done. I would've come up and gotten you."

She raised one of her crutches. "Going down was a lot easier than going up."

"Here," he said, running over to the breakfast table and pulling out a chair. "Have a seat. I'll get you something to drink and then set the table."

"Is there anything I can do to help? I can chop something," she said, sitting back and lifting her injured foot onto another one of the chairs.

"There's really nothing left to do. The risotto and the chicken are both ready. I just have to pull the roasted tomatoes out of the oven and we're good to go." He found a couple of bottles of Christmas Grove root beer in her refrigerator and placed them on the table.

"Risotto, chicken, and roasted tomatoes?" Holly let out a bark of laughter. "What? No dessert? Like a seven-layer cake or red velvet cheesecake? You know, something super easy to throw together."

It was his turn to laugh. "Funny. No, I haven't made dessert. Baking isn't exactly my specialty, but maybe we can work on something together after dinner."

"Oh! Christmas cookies. I even bought a fresh stash of sprinkles," she said, her smile wide and her eyes sparkling with excitement.

"Christmas cookies it is." Rex plated their food, and when he sat at the table with her, he couldn't remember a time when he'd felt more content. The time he'd spent in the kitchen had relaxed him, and the idea of making cookies with her sounded just about perfect. He picked up his fork and waited while she took the first bite.

Holly's eyes closed, and she let out a little moan of satisfaction as she savored the risotto. "Oh. Em. Gee," she said, her eyelids fluttering open. "Are you a trained chef or something? This is incredible."

"My dad liked to cook," he said, ignoring the flash of pain that always came when he talked about his father. Instead he focused on the sense of pride he felt at her obvious enjoyment. "So, is it safe to say you like it, then?"

"Like? No. Not even close." Shaking her head, she put her fork down, leaned in, and met his gaze as she added, "I love it. In fact, I'm trying to figure out how to hire you to fix all my meals for me for the next month. Between my ankle, the library, and planning the toy drive celebration, I don't know how I'm going to manage it all and get my holiday shopping done. I knew I should've started last month."

"No need to hire me. I'll happily volunteer," he said without hesitation. "It's better than eating alone, or worse, with Zach, whose ugly mug I already have to look at all day long." Rex would much rather spend his evenings with Holly, especially if he had the opportunity to dazzle her with his cooking skills.

"You can't be serious," she said, eyeing him with suspicion. "You're going to cook for me for free?"

"Well, not exactly free. I do expect to eat with you, so it's not like I'll be your personal chef or anything. Just think of me as your favorite neighbor who can't help but dazzle you with his cooking skills. And I'll even be your holiday shopping partner. I haven't started either."

She snorted out a laugh. "You don't really *like* shopping, do you? Is that just a ploy to spend more time with me?"

"Yes... and no." He grinned at her. "I really do need to get my shopping done, and to be honest, I could use some help. I'm certain my sister has exchanged every gift I've ever gotten her for the past fifteen years."

"That bad, huh?" Holly loaded another forkful of risotto. "So, this will be a mutually beneficial partnership? You cook for me, and I consult on your shopping?"

"Exactly. Deal?" He lifted his root beer bottle, waiting for her to do the same.

"Deal." Her entire face lit up as she clinked her bottle to his. "But let's go with mutually beneficial friendship."

"Friendship it is." He took a long pull of his root beer and decided that spending time in Christmas Grove was just about the best decision he'd made all year.

An hour later, with the dishes done and fresh sugar cookie dough stashed in the refrigerator, Rex followed Holly into her sitting room, holding two cups of decaf coffee.

"I think I'll bake the cookies tomorrow. And then if you want, we can decorate them before the mini golf date," Holly said as she eased herself onto her green velvet couch. She reached for a remote and after one click, the Christmas tree standing by her front window lit up with an abundance of clear lights. "What do you say? Will Zach let you off work an hour or so early?"

"Don't worry about Zach. He'll be too busy trying to figure out how to not mess up this date to care what I'm up to," Rex said with a chuckle. When Zach found out Rex was going to be decorating Christmas cookies, he was probably going to be too busy laughing his ass off to say anything about cutting out of work early. Besides, Rex wasn't an hourly employee. He was there to treat a section of the trees on the farm. It wasn't exactly a nine to five job. Rex handed Holly her coffee and took a seat at the other end of her couch.

"Seriously?" Holly asked, twisting toward him. "I thought this date was Ilsa's idea. You mean he really likes her?"

Oops. He'd said more than he should've when it came to Zach and Ilsa. "I think he's had his eye on her for a while. But do you mind keeping it to yourself? He hasn't actually come out and said anything, but I've known Zach a long time, and there's no way he's not into her."

"I see." Holly chuckled. "Well, at least they seem to be on the same page then. Hopefully they can figure it out."

Rex leaned back into the cushions, resting his arm along the back of the sofa. "Enough about them. I want to learn more about you, Holly. How did you end up living alone in this giant Victorian?"

She glanced around, seeming to take in the details of her old home. Everything about her softened, her smile, her eyes, the set of her shoulders. "It was my grandmother's. She left it to me when she passed ten years ago. It's sometimes a little much to maintain, but I don't mind at all. Living here makes me feel close to her."

He knew that already. Zach had filled him in. He'd actually been trying to fish around to find out why she wasn't paired up with somebody. But the way she talked about her grandmother, the love and reverence, made him curious about the other aspects of her life. "It sounds like you had a special relationship with her. Did you spend a lot of time here while you were growing up?"

Some of the softness fled as a cloudy expression flashed in her eyes. "I lived with her after my parents died."

Oh hell. That was something he hadn't known. Zach had given him the barest of details it seemed. "I'm sorry. Both of them? Was it an accident?"

She nodded. "Their private plane went down when they were on the way from the Keys to New York. I was fourteen. That's when I moved to Christmas Grove to live with Gran."

He reached out and squeezed her hand. "That's rough."

Holly curled her fingers around his, but then quickly withdrew and straightened her shoulders as if she were steeling herself against pain she wouldn't let herself wallow in. "It was, because I lost them. And that was horrible. But eventually it wasn't. I love Christmas Grove, and Gran was the best. I spent most of my summers here and any time my parents were traveling, so it was already a second home. All things considered I think I was pretty lucky."

"Do you have other family nearby?" he asked.

She shook her head. "I have cousins back east. They're from Dad's stepbrother who was ten years older than him. I met them once when I was really little. He and Dad weren't close. Mom was Gran's only child."

Rex let her words sink in. The beautiful creature sitting opposite him didn't have any family left, or at least any that meant something to her. No wonder she'd been so adamant about not dating anyone temporary. All of the people she'd loved most had left her. He decided right then and there that no matter how attracted he was to her, he wasn't going to push it. They'd be *friends*, just like she'd asked.

CHAPTER 5

"*W*hat about you, Rex. Do you have family?" Holly asked curiously. She barely knew anything about the man other than he was friends with Zach, an earth witch, and seriously sexy. Not to mention kind and generous.

He nodded. "Yeah. A big one. Two moms, a stepdad, and ten siblings. My bio dad passed when I was a teenager."

Holly didn't miss the flash of pain in his eyes when he mentioned his biological father. "I'm sorry about your dad. I know how hard it is."

He just nodded and glanced away. Clearly, he didn't want to talk about it. She understood completely.

"So, blended family?" she asked, having no clue what it would be like to be related to that many people. It sounded both wonderfully delightful and frighteningly overwhelming.

"Yep. My parents divorced when I was five and Amelia was three. They both remarried within a couple of years, resulting in an additional five half-brothers and four half-sisters. Dad had three more while Mom had six, including the final set of triplets. And believe it or not, my mom is best friends with my stepmom, so we always celebrate everything together. Holidays are a zoo."

"Wait. Your mom's best friend married your dad? Didn't that result in a lot of drama?" she asked, astonished.

Rex let out a bark of laughter. "No, not at all. They became friends after everyone was remarried. It's not as weird as it sounds. After Dad..." He swallowed. "After we lost him, Georgie really leaned on Mom. My parents' divorce was mostly amicable, so there never was any jealousy. Mom was glad Dad was happy and vice versa. It's actually really nice that all of the kids feel like family, even though Amelia and I are the only ones related to all of them."

Holly covered his hand with hers and squeezed lightly. "That sounds wonderful, Rex. I've never had anything close to that."

"It can be fantastic," he admitted. "But it's also easy to sort of get lost in the shuffle. Amelia and I are pretty close, though. We always know when the other one needs to be found."

The softness in his tone touched Holly. It was obvious he loved his sister very much. "Where is she now? New York?"

He nodded. "She works for the fire department. Pretty cliché for a fire witch, right?"

"Sounds practical to me," Holly said. "And the fire department is lucky to have her." Every fire department actively looked to staff at least one fire witch. They had the skills to control and tamp down a fire, making them invaluable.

"They are. She's really powerful, too." There was undeniable pride in his voice. "It's been a while since I've seen her. It's one of the reasons I took the job in New York. I wanted to spend more time with her besides the sporadic trips we try to throw together once a year."

"So, you're a traveler, too?" Holly asked, trying to ignore the sudden anxiety building in her chest. It didn't occur to her to wonder why she was feeling that way. The answer was obvious. She liked Rex Holiday more than was good for her. And besides the fact that he was moving to New York, if he was a man who liked to see the world, there would be no denying they weren't compatible.

Holly had once wanted to go everywhere and see everything. The thought of exploring all the corners of the world had been her dream. Her parents had always been going on trips that sounded so exciting to her. Paris, Amsterdam, the Florida Keys, Costa Rica, Spain, anywhere that caught their fancy. But after they died, her wanderlust had died right along with them. It was as if she'd grown roots in Christmas Grove. She was comfortable there. Her grandmother's house was there. She had Ilsa and the rest of the town who loved her. Leaving just wasn't in the cards for her. Not even to see the Eiffel tower.

"I guess you could call me a traveler," Rex said, pinching his brows together as he formulated his answer. "I move around a lot. Going from job to job. My line of work requires me to go to the farmer, you know?"

"Of course. Makes sense," she said, still trying to figure out why she was so upset by his answer. It wasn't as if she had plans to be in a relationship with the guy. She'd known from the beginning that he was temporary. This getting to know him and going on a date was just for fun. She deserved to enjoy herself, didn't she? Even if she knew it was going absolutely nowhere?

"Right. Anyway," he continued, "because I'm on the move for work so much, I don't actually vacation all that often. It's rare for me to plan a trip somewhere other than my sister's house. She keeps a room for me there. If she wants a getaway, sometimes we get a beach condo somewhere on the east coast, though she did come out here once. That's just so we can relax and catch up. We don't actually do a lot of sightseeing. Mostly I drink beer while she drinks wine, and we fill each other in on who we've dated, who we've kicked to the curb, and what's going on in our lives. You know, sibling stuff."

She didn't know, though. She was an only child. "That sounds a lot like the stuff Ilsa and I talk about."

"Right." Amusement lit his gaze as he added, "But with Amelia and me, I'm sure there's a lot more ribbing going on. We excel at giving each other hell."

"Sibling rivalry. I've seen it in action with Ilsa and her brother. Always fascinating, considering I've never had that experience. I guess you'll be going to her house for Christmas then?" she asked, trying to sound casual. She thought she'd succeeded but then realized she was fidgeting with one of the corded edges of a pillow, making her look anxious. *Dammit.* Why did she care if he was around for Christmas? She'd be with Ilsa and her family like always.

"Actually, no. This year my mom and stepdad are going on a Paris holiday, and my stepmom has a new boyfriend who is taking her to the Caribbean. So everyone has decided to do their own thing, and Amelia chose to come out here."

"That's great. I can't wait to meet her." Holly internally winced. Had she really just said that? It sounded as if it was a given. Well, it might as well be. If she and Rex were going to be friends, then it would make sense she'd meet his sister. Right? She covered her mouth and yawned so hard her eyes started to water.

"You two will love each other," he said as he stood. "Looks

like I need to get out of here and let you get some sleep. Need help getting upstairs?"

Yes. There was nothing she wanted more than to feel his arms around her again as he carried her to her bedroom. But that was just a recipe for a disaster. "No thanks. I'm probably going to just sleep down here in the guest room. The guest bathroom is stocked with extra toiletries, and lucky for me, I haven't hauled my clean laundry upstairs. I'll be fine."

He gave her a skeptical look but finally said, "Hand me your phone."

She blinked. "Why? Do you need to call someone?"

His lips twitched into a half smile. "Yeah. You later to check on you. Hand it over. I'm going to text myself so we can exchange numbers."

Oh. Right. "Sure." She pulled her phone out of her pocket, unlocked it, and handed it over.

A few moments later, she heard a text notification come from his phone in his pocket, and he handed her phone back to her. "I programmed my number into your contacts. Please call me if you need anything. Anything at all. I'm not crazy about leaving you here alone."

"I will. I promise," she said, wondering if that were the truth. She'd probably call Ilsa first, but it didn't hurt to have backup. Especially when the backup was gorgeous. She swallowed a groan and pushed herself up onto her good foot.

"You didn't need to get up," Rex said, moving into her personal space.

She stared into his bright blue eyes. "I just wanted to say goodnight."

"Goodnight," he whispered as he leaned in closer.

Whoa. What was happening here? Was he going to kiss her? She stood there frozen like a deer in headlights as he brushed his lips lightly over her cheek and then wrapped his arms around her, hugging her tightly.

"I had a good time getting to know you," he said into her ear. "I'm glad we get to do it again tomorrow."

"Me, too," she admitted.

He pressed his lips to her cheek one last time before striding out of her front door into the moonlit night.

CHAPTER 6

"*I* can't believe you two are going to sit here making goo-goo eyes at each other while I make a fool of myself in front of Zack," Ilsa hissed as she flattened both of her palms on the table and leaned in closer. "You were supposed to be my wingman and wingwoman."

"You don't need a wingman," Rex said, leaning back into his chair and draping a casual arm over Holly's shoulders. "Just be yourself. It'll be fine."

Holly's neck and spine started to tingle from the contact. Did he have any idea what he was doing to her? They were sitting at an outside table at Karma Arcade, watching as Ilsa and Zach made their way around the mini golf course.

"Hols," Ilsa pleaded. "You have to hobble over to the next hole and help me out. I'm dying. You should hear our stilted conversation. I sound like an idiot."

"I'm sure you don't. I've never heard you sound like an idiot your entire life," Holly said, glancing over to where Zach was standing and holding two golf putters. "He appears to be happy enough. Look at that smile on his face. It just got wider when his eyes landed on you," she said to Ilsa. "Stop worrying. You've got this."

Ilsa glanced nervously over at Zach while fidgeting with the hem of her shirt, and Holly wondered what the heck was going on. Ilsa was the most confident person she knew. The girl flirted with the best of them. All the time. Holly couldn't remember a single instance when her friend didn't know how to talk her way in or out of anything. But right at that moment, she was completely off her game. "Whatever crazy shit you're telling yourself," Holly said, "forget it right this minute. Do you understand me? Go back over there and flirt with that man like I know you can. Like you have a million times before."

"I'm not telling myself anything," Ilsa said, raising her chin and glancing away.

"Oh, just stop it right now. Don't lie to your best friend. I can see right through you."

They'd been at the Karma Arcade for less than thirty minutes, and Ilsa was ready to bolt. Holly could see it in her eyes. "Is this why you made sure it was a double date? Are you that nervous?"

"Yes. I thought that was obvious," she said. "I can't do this. I'm going to do or say something really stupid and—"

"Ilsa," Holly said, grabbing her friend by the shoulders. "It's just Zach. You've known him for years. Heck, you've flirted with him for years. Relax, okay? He already knows you. And you already know him. If he didn't like you, he wouldn't have agreed to this date."

The dark-haired woman smoothed her hair down and squared her shoulders as she glanced at Holly and Rex again. "So, you're really staying here then?"

Rex raised his Irish coffee while Holly repeated the gesture with her eggnog.

"Fine. But if I die of embarrassment, it's both of your faults." She whipped around, tossing her hair over one shoulder, and headed back to Zach, where she shoved her hands in her pockets and followed him to the next hole.

"Is she always like that?" Rex asked, studying Holly's best friend.

"No. Never," Holly said with a laugh. "Usually she's really sassy and confident, but there's something about Zach tonight that's putting her off-kilter."

"I see." There was humor in Rex's expression as he watched them bicker over the best way to line up a shot. "She must *really* like him then."

"Or he just gets under her skin," Holly said, not wanting to betray her friend's confidence. Though it was fairly obvious that Rex was right. Ilsa couldn't keep her eyes off Zach as he carefully lined up his putter and sent the ball straight into the opening of the red and green windmill.

"He definitely gets under her skin," Rex said with a nod. "The funny part is that he doesn't seem to realize that."

Holly squinted as she watched Zach. He glanced over his shoulder and smiled at Ilsa when his golf ball bounced out of the windmill and ended up a few inches from the hole. Ilsa rolled her eyes and clucked her tongue. She said something that made him throw his head back and laugh, but Holly couldn't hear it. Instead, she watched as her friend turned bright red and started stammering.

"Oh no," Holly said, her heart going out to her friend. "She must've said something super embarrassing." After downing the rest of her eggnog in one gulp, Holly stood and grabbed her crutches. "I need to save her from herself."

Rex stood too, eyeing her foot. "How's the ankle?"

"It hasn't hurt at all since I drank that pain potion first

thing this morning, but I can feel a twinge if I try to put much pressure on it. As long as I lean on the crutch, it should be fine." She twisted around and expertly crutched her way over to her friend. "Hey," she said. "What happened?"

"Oh gods," Ilsa whispered. "I just told him I'm impressed with how he handled his balls."

"What?" Holly asked, unable to stop her bark of laughter. "Why did you say that?"

"I meant shots, but it came out balls. He's really good at this. But why the hell did I say balls? There's something seriously wrong with me."

"No there isn't. You're just nervous." Holly glanced over at Zach and Rex. They had their heads huddled together and were chuckling. No doubt, it was at Ilsa's expense. Not that she could blame them. If the shoe were on the other foot, she and Ilsa would be laughing their asses off, too. She turned her attention back to her friend. "Okay. Calm down. I'm here now. Why don't you take your shot, and I'll get Rex to find us some clubs and golf balls so we can join you."

"All right." Ilsa sucked in a long breath and created a puff of steam when she let it out. The night was on the chilly side, but they'd dressed for it and were warm enough in their wool coats and knitted hats. Ilsa dropped her red ball onto the putting green, lined up, and swung with all her force at the windmill.

The ball flew through the air so quickly that Holly didn't even it see it bounce off of one of the blades and fly right back at her, slamming into the crutch she was leaning on and knocking it out of her grasp.

"Whoa!" Holly cried as she fell flat on her back right there on the putting green.

"Holy hell!" Ilsa cried, slamming her palm over her open

mouth. She muttered something that Holly couldn't understand.

"What?" Holly asked, mentally taking inventory of her poor body. The only pain she felt was a dull ache from getting the wind knocked out of her. She wiggled her fingers and toes, making sure everything was working.

"I'm so sorry, Hols," Ilsa said, kneeling beside Holly. "Ohmigod, I shouldn't be allowed out of the house until after the Mercury in retrograde passes. I'm a walking disaster!"

"No, you aren't," Zach said, pulling her up and wrapping his arms around her. "You just got overzealous with your need to beat me at mini golf."

Ilsa froze and stared at her date, seemingly speechless. Then she glanced down at Holly. "I'm so sorry."

"It's not your fault," Holly said, trying to let her friend off the hook. Because who were they kidding? It was Ilsa's fault. She was the one who whacked the crap out of that ball, causing it to fly way too high and way too fast for a putt-putt game. But she knew Ilsa would rather blacken her own eye before she hurt anyone else.

"It is my fault," Ilsa insisted. No one argued with her this time.

"Holly?" Rex dropped the clubs he'd acquired from the front office and squatted down beside her. His forehead was creased in worry. "Are you all right? Do I need to get you back to the healer?"

There was so much concern in his tone that it made Holly's chest ache with longing. Was that what it felt like to have a partner? Someone to take care of her when she needed someone to lean on? She'd barely known him for two days, and already she was dreading the day when he left for New York.

"I'm fine," Holly said, rubbing her chest over her heart. "Just got the wind knocked out of me." She pushed herself into an upright position, checking each of her limbs to make sure she wasn't having a delayed reaction.

"Come here," Rex said, bending down to help lift her up onto her uninjured foot.

"Thanks," she breathed, enjoying the small tingle of magic that slipped from his fingertips when he touched her.

"I think we should probably get you home," he said. Then he turned to Zack and Ilsa, who had broken apart and were standing there looking awkward. "Don't worry about us. You two enjoy the rest of your night."

"But how will you get home?" Ilsa asked. "We all came in one car."

"I'm sure he can figure it out," Zack said, placing a hand on her hip.

"But—" Ilsa started.

"We'll find a ride," Holly said, grateful that Rex was taking charge and getting her out of there. She was thoroughly done with the mini golf course.

"Okay." Ilsa bit down on her lower lip and then mouthed, *Sorry.*

Holly waved a hand, indicating she shouldn't worry about it. "Have fun," she said, taking the crutch Rex had retrieved for her. "Don't worry about us. We still have a dozen Christmas cookies to finish decorating." Rex had been held up at the farm, so their plans to finish the cookies before the date hadn't panned out.

"Christmas cookies?" Ilsa parroted.

Holly pretended she hadn't heard her and crutched her way into the arcade and out onto Main Street with Rex at her side.

"Well. That was different," Holly said with a laugh as Rex

scrolled through his phone. "Think they'll find their rhythm now that it's just them?"

"I hope so." He glanced over at her. "How do you feel about a carriage ride around town before I get you home?"

Holly felt her lips split into a pleased smile. "That sounds wonderful. I've been wanting to see all the Christmas lights but haven't had a chance to cruise around yet."

"Are you sure you're okay? That fall back there—"

"I'm okay," she insisted, rolling her shoulders to make sure she hadn't developed any aches or pains from the fall. "It just surprised me. I'm fine. Really."

"Good." He wrapped an arm around her shoulders and pulled her in for a soft, sideways hug. "I wasn't ready for the night to be over just yet."

She leaned into him and felt her insides turn to goo. There was nothing she wanted more than to cuddle up next to him as they toured the streets of Christmas Grove in one of the magical horseless carriages. *Oh hell*, she thought. *I'm doomed.*

CHAPTER 7

*R*ex helped Holly into the white, open-air horseless carriage. He followed her and sat on the red velvet bench seat as she covered them both with the plush blanket the carriage company supplied to keep them warm.

"Good evening, Mr. Holiday," a voice said out of nowhere. "Which tour may I take you and your companion on tonight?"

"The holiday lights tour, please," Rex said.

"It would be my pleasure." The carriage rolled forward, heading down Main Street. Twinkle lights glowed from the lampposts, and soft instrumental Christmas music filled the night. "If you would like to stop anywhere for a closer look, just say, *stop*. And when you're ready to resume, say, *carry on*," the voice instructed.

"You know what?" Holly asked.

Rex turned his attention to her, loving the sparkle in her eyes. "What's that?"

"In all the years I've lived here in Christmas Grove, I've never taken a carriage tour. Can you believe that?"

"Seriously?" Rex scooted a little closer so he could drape his

45

arm around her shoulder. "Are you really telling me that none of your boyfriends were romantic enough to take you on a Christmas lights tour?"

She barked out a laugh. "Well, there have only been two boyfriends, and one wasn't here during Christmas time. And the other... Let's just say that his idea of a perfect day involved something like snowboarding or spending half the night at the local pub. Sitting still for a carriage ride definitely wasn't ever going to be on his radar."

"Amateur." Rex scoffed, wondering what was wrong with the second guy. That didn't sound like dating. It was more like hanging with a buddy. "There's no way to hold your date when you're flying down the slopes on a piece of fiberglass."

She laughed. "You're not wrong. But we were young. Just out of high school. What do you expect?"

"Even in high school I knew better than that," Rex insisted. The memory of him renting a snowmobile to take Sara on their first date to the skating rink out near the lake in their small town in upstate New York flashed in his mind. The night had been perfect. First she'd wrapped her arms tightly around him on the snowmobile, and then he'd kept an arm around her as they inched their way across the ice skating rink. He'd spent most of the night with her body pressed against his. At seventeen, everything about the night had been glorious.

"What's that look on your face?" Holly asked.

"What look?" he asked, meeting her pretty green eyes.

"That smirk combined with your narrowed eyes makes you look both smug and annoyed."

"Oh. That look." He chuckled. "I was just thinking about a high school date. I did everything I could to guarantee she'd have to put her arms around me. Snowmobile and ice skating. Perfect combo, right?"

Her lips twitched with amusement. "That explains the smugness. What about that annoyed you?"

He shrugged, not wanting to talk about Sara. The memories of her always put him in a bad mood. But as they rolled down a residential street that was lit up with thousands of Christmas lights, Rex wondered if he finally talked about that night when everything went to hell if he might be able to finally let it all go. "That date was with Sara, my ex fiancée," he blurted. "She... ended up not being a good person."

Holly reached over and placed her hand over his, squeezing his fingers. "I'm sorry. How long were you two together?"

"Six years. She was not who I thought she was," he said, turning his head to gaze at a house that had a lit-up replica of Santa and his eight reindeer.

"Do you want to tell me about it?" she asked, her voice barely a whisper.

"Not really." He turned his attention to her again, the story right on the tip of his tongue. But he swallowed it. He didn't want to ruin his date with her by pouring out his sob story. Besides, that was a long time ago. "It doesn't matter now anyway."

"It matters if her memory still bothers you," Holly said. There wasn't any judgment in her tone, just understanding. It made him wonder what stories she was keeping to herself. She threaded her fingers through his and added, "You can talk to me, Rex. We're friends, remember? Besides, you'll be leaving in January. Whatever this is between us, we both know it's temporary. And maybe someone who's temporary is just the right kind of person to spill your guts to."

Except he didn't want her to be temporary. The thought slammed him in the gut. He'd known he was interested in her from the moment he first saw her, but every time she talked about him leaving Christmas Grove, his stomach twisted in knots. That implied more than just a passing interest. He wanted more. So much more. He wanted someone who was kind, smart, and grounded. Holly Reineer was all of those things and more. And for some reason, he wanted her to know his story. He sighed and muttered, "Oh, hell."

"What is it, Rex?" she asked, sounding worried. "Is something wrong?"

"No," he answered quickly. "I was just thinking about what happened with Sara. Have you ever loved someone enough that you wanted to marry them?"

"Yes," she said, not meeting his eyes. The disappointment in her voice matched the disappointment Rex had carried with him for the past ten years.

"Did you ever actually get engaged?" he asked as the carriage rolled by city hall. He pointed to the animated replicas of Santa and Mrs. Claus that were dancing in the gazebo out front.

Her face lit up as she smiled at the scene. When she glanced back at him, she shook her head. "No. Though he was supposed to come back and propose at Christmas two years ago."

"He didn't, I take it," Rex asked.

"Nope. He didn't even bother to call me. I got a note in the mail with an apology. He said he just wasn't ready and that he'd be back someday for me, but he won't. My visions say otherwise. Besides, did he really think I was just going to wait here in Christmas Grove, pining away, until he finally decides he can't live without me? Not likely."

"He sent you a note?" Rex gaped at her. "Really?"

"Really. It was a Christmas card, too. The front said *Have a Very Merry Christmas*. Inside he wrote that he wasn't ready, but that he'd be back for me one day. I burned it, along with some sage to clear his energy."

"Did the sage work?" he asked, hoping to hell it had. He didn't want her heart pining for some guy who cared so little for her that he'd broken things off with her in a Christmas card.

"Somewhat." She shrugged. "I've let him go if that's what you mean."

Relief filtered through him as his shoulders relaxed. It was interesting that he hadn't even realized how much he'd needed to hear her say that. "That's good. If I had a space to smudge, maybe I'd give it a go."

Holly's expression turned sympathetic. "Do you still miss her?"

"What?" he asked, surprised at the question. "Oh. No. I'd use the sage to clear the bad energy, that's all. Trust me. I don't have anything left for Sara other than resentment. It was six years of my life that she threw away. It's hard not to feel resentful."

"There's quite the story there," she said. It was a statement, not a question.

"Yeah. Definitely." It was nearly impossible to not feel hostile when talking about Sara. She'd not only betrayed him; she'd also stolen something vital in him that he'd never gotten back. "I proposed five years to the day of our first date. We were right back at that same ice skating rink. I got down on one knee right in the middle of the ice and asked her if she'd be my wife." The pain of the memory almost took his breath away. How could he have been such a fool? "Tears ran down her face as she said yes. I was the happiest man in the world that day."

Holly stiffened, and he wondered what she was thinking.

After a moment, she cleared her throat as she asked, "What happened?"

A storm built inside of Rex as he worked up the nerve to say the words he'd never told anyone before... not even Amelia. "We were supposed to get married that same day one year later. A week before the wedding, I found her in bed with her best guy friend. And they weren't just cuddling."

Holly's eyes widened in shock, and she shook her head as if to deny that someone could be so hurtful. "Oh my god," she whispered. "How awful for you."

"It gets worse," Rex continued as bile rose up to the back of his throat. The flood gates had been opened, and now after keeping Sara's betrayal to himself for a decade, he had to get it out, tell someone, tell *her*. He had no idea why he'd decided she was the one he could confide in, but he couldn't hold back now if he tried. There was an ache in his gut, and instinctively he knew it wouldn't go away until he spoke his truth. "She and Josh, that was her friend, had been having a sexual relationship the entire time we were together."

"That's... terrible, Rex." She squeezed his hand, holding on so tight, he thought his fingers might go numb. But he welcomed the pressure. It seemed to help ground him. "I'm so sorry," she added. "I can't believe she was cheating on you all those years and still thought it was a good idea to get married."

"Neither could I, to be honest," he said, rubbing his chest with his free hand. Even after all these years, he could still feel the ache in his chest he'd felt that day when he realized everything they'd had was a complete lie. "You want to know what's worse?"

"I can't imagine what's worse than finding out your fiancée is cheating on you," she said quietly.

"I actually asked her if we could work it out." Rex hung his head, not wanting her to see his burning cheeks. He was embarrassed at how blind he'd been.

"She didn't want to?" Holly asked.

"Oh, she did," he said and snorted with disgust. "She said she wanted an open relationship because she had a connection with Josh she just didn't have with me. But even that was a lie. I found out later she was just planning to marry me for the modest trust fund my dad left me when he died. She never loved me. Last I heard, she'd married Josh and they were selling some get-rich-quick scheme on the internet."

"Holy hell, Rex," Holly breathed. "You never once suspected?"

He raised his head and looked her straight in the eye. "Not once. We didn't live together, so she had her privacy to do what she wanted when she was on her own. We were both really independent. It was one of the things that attracted me to her. It took me a long time to accept that Sara had no conscience and that I was played."

"It's a damned good thing you walked in on them that day, Rex," she said. "Imagine what would've happened if you'd actually married her."

He shuddered at the thought. Instead of just being embarrassed and heartbroken, he would've had a major legal mess on his hands, too. "You're right of course. You could say she really did a number on me."

"Anyone would be messed up after the one person they trusted most turned out to be a fraud," she said, scooting closer to him. "But, Rex?"

He turned to her, forcing himself to meet her gaze. He needed to know if she thought less of him for being duped by a con artist. But all he saw in her expression was compassion and understanding.

"You didn't do anything wrong. What happened with Sara, that's all on her. She's the one who should be embarrassed by her behavior, not you."

"I'm not embarrassed," he lied and grimaced. His cheeks were still hot, and there was no doubt he was flushed.

She pressed her lips to his cheek and murmured, "Good. Because I see pure love and strength when I look at you."

While he appreciated her words, he couldn't agree. But he needed to move on from this conversation. Talking about Sara had put him on edge. So instead of listing the reasons she was wrong, he just said, "Thank you. That's kind of you to say."

"It's not kind, Rex. It's the truth."

CHAPTER 8

*H*olly understood that Rex had no idea what she meant when she'd said she saw love and strength when she looked at him. It was obvious by the way he'd quickly changed the subject and started asking about the toy drive that was coming up.

"Is there anything I can do to help?" he asked.

"Sure. You can help me collect them from Lemon at Christmas Grove Express. I'll need a truck, and since you have one…"

"Done." He grinned at her. "Just tell me when."

That right there, his willingness to jump in and help wherever he was needed, was the love she was talking about. Rex Holiday had a huge heart that was obvious to everyone but himself. Look at how he'd been with her when she hurt her foot, and that they were in a carriage at that very moment because he'd stepped in after Ilsa had laid her out flat. "You're a good man, Rex."

"Nah. I'm just a dude with a truck who wants to spend

more time with a pretty girl." He winked at her, and it was as if the conversation about his ex-fiancée had never happened.

She rolled her eyes. "You didn't have to volunteer to help with the toy drive for that. You're making me dinner every night, remember?"

He laughed. "Right. You're gonna miss me once the holidays are over and you have to go back to making yourself sandwiches and mac and cheese."

She knew he was teasing, but that didn't stop the clench of her gut when he reminded her he was leaving. That had to stop. She couldn't keep getting upset over the inevitable. At some point, her visceral reaction needed to chill out. He was her friend. And that was all he was going to be. "You're going to miss my cookies," she said. "And wait until you taste my berry pie. You're going to weep when you get to New York and realize nothing comes close."

He threw his head back and laughed. "You know, you're probably right. Maybe I can get you to give me some baking lessons. Then I can at least try to emulate your magic."

"You want to learn to bake? For real?" she asked, tilting her head to study him.

"If you're teaching, sure. I've had a craving for those peanut butter cookies with chocolate kisses. Maybe we could start there." He pointed to a large house to the right and said, "Stop, please." The carriage slowed and came to a stop, just as promised.

Holly glanced over and gasped when she spotted the elaborate Whoville village in the front yard, complete with a Grinch on the roof.

"Look across the street," Rex said.

But Holly was too busy gaping at the whimsical

gingerbread type houses to care what the neighbors had come up with.

"Snoopy is getting ready to do his double axel," Rex said.

"What?" Holly twisted around and gasped as she watched an animated Snoopy spin around in the air and land perfectly on one skate. The entire Peanuts gang were there on a small skating rink. Off to the side, there was a red doghouse that was decorated with Christmas lights and a few bulbs. It had a First Prize ribbon on it. "Oh, my goodness. The town has gone all out this year!"

"Is there a competition or something?" Rex asked.

Holly nodded. "Sure. There always is. I haven't really checked what the prizes are this year. It must be something really great considering the effort everyone is putting in. I guess I'll have to take a look."

"I could help you decorate your house if you want to enter," he said. "If that's something you're into. If not, you can just show me your secret pie recipe instead."

"Pie. Right," she said, rolling her eyes even as a grin claimed her lips. "If you want my recipes, you'll have to come join my baking class on Wednesday nights down at Charming Cookie's"

"That bakery on the square?" he asked, his eyes lit with interest. "You actually teach once a week?"

"Yes, and yes," she said, suddenly feeling shy. Holly learned everything she knew from her grandmother, who'd once made a living taking special orders for parties and celebrations. The woman could've had a shop with lines out the door if she'd wanted, but she preferred to set her own hours and only take on the work she wanted to do. It wasn't long after her gran passed that Cookie Kelly opened Charming Cookie's and filled the void that Holly's gran had left.

"Do I need to sign up for my spot, or is it drop in?" he asked.

"Either. If you want a dedicated station, sign up. But if you just drop in, you can share mine." Oh, hell. Why had she said that? She'd share her station? She never did that. But it didn't matter. She was certain he'd only been flirting anyway. The likelihood of him showing up for an actual class was probably pretty slim.

"Perfect. Wednesday night. Got it. Now, about decorating your Victorian. The offer is still on the table. I'm not an air witch, but I'm good with my hands."

Holly's gaze immediately fell to his hand that was resting on his knee. She'd been imagining what those hands might be able to do. A shiver of desire ran through her, and she had to look away just to calm down. *Deep breaths, Reineer,* she told herself. She couldn't go mauling the man right there on the street. It was indecent. But what about when they got to her house? Would she invite him in? They did still have a batch of Christmas cookies to decorate. She couldn't exactly just send him on his way. She sneaked another glance at his hand.

Rex laughed.

"What?" she asked him.

"Nothing." But the sly grin on his face told her he'd known exactly what she was thinking. Her face burned with heat, but she didn't turn away. Instead she leaned in, brushing her lips against his cheek, and whispered, "I was just wondering how many Christmas trees I could get you to set up in my front yard with those hands. And just what I'd have to do to get you to wrap them with twinkle lights."

He sucked in a breath. "How many trees?"

"Seven? Nine? I'm not sure. Enough to recreate the Great Hall scene at Christmas time from Harry Potter." She grinned.

"You said you'd help decorate my yard. I've always wanted a Hogwarts scene. I don't have the magic to pull it off though. We'll need an air witch to deal with all the floating candles."

"I know just the witch," he said. "Don't give it another thought. By tomorrow night you won't even recognize your place." He took that big hand of his that had been resting on his knee and moved it to hers, squeezing lightly.

Everything inside of her tingled from his touch. Holy hell. If he kept that up, they for sure wouldn't be decorating cookies when they got back to her place. They'd be lucky to make it upstairs before she was ripping his clothes off. Rex Holiday was pushing all of her buttons.

"Carry on," he said and sat back, pulling her with him as the carriage once again started to roll.

"Stop," Rex said when they were halfway down the driveway to the Victorian. He pointed to the clearing that had once been used as a pumpkin patch but was now just overflow parking for customers during berry season. "There. That's where we put the Great Hall."

"You're right. That's probably the best place. The actual front yard is a little small," Holly agreed.

"We could put up an event tent, and even build an arch to make it look like the inside of the castle," he said, eyeing the clearing.

"You're really into this idea, aren't you?" Holly asked with a laugh, not at all sure he was serious. "I mean, I know it's Hogwarts and all, but that's a lot of work for a place that isn't even yours. I'm not going to hold you to this."

"What?" he asked, pulling back and pressing his palm to

his chest, feigning offense. "I was looking forward to living out my childhood fantasy with the sorting hat. You can't take that away from me now. I've already mentally drawn the plans."

Shaking her head, she said, "You're a bigger Potter fan than I am, I think."

"What can I say? I'm still waiting for that owl to bring me my Hogwarts acceptance letter."

She giggled. "Honestly, me too."

"So, it's on then? We'll create our own Hogwarts Christmas right here?" he asked.

"Of course. If we can find an air witch willing to spell hundreds of candles. It won't be right without floating candles," she said, already imagining spending Christmas Eve in the Great Hall.

"I've got it covered." He turned his attention toward the house. "Carry on." The carriage rolled on and stopped in front of her porch. "You wait here," he told Holly as he hopped to the ground. "I'll help you down."

"I can get out. I just—" she started.

"Nope. I don't want you slipping and hurting your foot again," he said, already reaching up for her from her side of the carriage.

"All right. Help me out of this thing," she said, thoroughly enjoying being taken care of. She'd never dated anyone so attentive before. It could've been annoying or even overwhelming, but when it was Rex ordering her to stay put so that he could lift her down, for some reason, she really didn't mind. Deep inside, she knew the reason, she just didn't want to admit that she liked him taking care of her. It was something she couldn't afford to get used to.

Rex grabbed her by the waist and gently lifted her out of

the carriage. After retrieving her crutches, he said, "Carry on," and the carriage took off down the driveway.

"Were you planning on staying?" she blurted, surprised that he'd sent off his only possibility for a ride back to town.

"Is that an invitation?" he asked, his eyes glinting with humor.

"Um, I..." She blew out a breath and finally said, "That's probably not a good idea."

Rex chuckled. "Right. To answer your question, no, I wasn't planning on staying too long. But we do need to finish those Christmas cookies waiting for us and then make sure you get upstairs without having to crutch your way to the top. Then I was going to walk home to my cabin."

"Oh. Of course," she said, feeling like an idiot. It made sense that he'd walk home. Zach's farm and the cabin Rex was staying in were right next door. She let out a nervous laugh. "I forgot you're staying so close."

He raised one eyebrow but didn't say another word as he followed her up the porch.

Once inside, Holly pressed her hand to her mouth, trying to stifle a huge yawn. It had been a long day of working at the library and then coming home to get ready for her date. She'd lied the night before when she said she had clean laundry downstairs, which meant she had to work her way to the second floor. She'd been more than winded by the time she made it into her bedroom.

"You look like you could use a good night's sleep," Rex said to her. "Want to finish the cookies tomorrow?"

"If we keep putting them off, they'll be stale by the time they get their sparkle," she said with a soft smile.

"Nah. They'll keep another day. Let me get you upstairs, and then I'll get out of your hair," he said.

She knew she should refuse. Tell him that she'd manage on her own. But as she opened her mouth to protest, the words didn't come. Instead, she said, "Thanks. That would really help."

So much for being the independent woman.

"Grab your crutches in one hand," he said.

Holly did as she was told, and a second later, Rex lifted her up and cradled her against his chest, just as he'd done the day before at the healer's office. Without another word, he effortlessly carried her up the stairs, but instead of putting her down in the hallway, he asked, "Which one is your room?"

"The one at the end of the hall," she said, her voice husky.

He tightened his grip on her, carried her into her room, and after taking her crutches from her and leaning them against the wall, he gently laid her down on her comfortable queen-size bed.

"You'll need to check on Sabrina for me before you go," she said, smiling up at him.

"Sabrina?"

"Our bunny. She's in the kitchen."

"*Our* bunny?" he asked, amusement in his blue gaze.

"Yeah. Our bunny. She misses you," Holly said, squeezing his fingers. "Thanks for tonight. I had a really nice time."

"So did I," he said, sitting beside her on the bed. "I guess we have Ilsa and Zach to thank for arranging it, huh?"

"The only thing I'm going to thank Ilsa for is sparing my face when she tried to kill me with a golf ball."

"Thank her for me, too," he said with a laugh. Then his expression turned serious as he gazed down at her. His eyes were searching and suddenly full of heat as they stared at each other.

Holly's breath caught. Her skin tingled, desperate to be

touched by him. The electricity sparking between them was off the charts, and when Rex lowered his head close to hers, she stopped breathing altogether. If he kissed her, all bets were off. There wasn't enough willpower in the world for her to send him away.

"Holly," he breathed.

"Yes?" she answered.

His lips brushed over her cheek and then lightly over her lips as he whispered, "Goodnight. I'll see you tomorrow night for dinner."

Then he was gone.

CHAPTER 9

$\mathcal{I}$t took every last bit of Rex's willpower to walk away from Holly. He wanted her. More than he'd ever wanted anyone in his life.

But she'd made it clear he wasn't invited. Or at least that's what she'd said when they were outside and she'd questioned how he was going to get home.

He hadn't missed the catch of her breath or the desire in her brilliant green eyes when he leaned down to kiss her goodnight. Rex was intuitive enough to know that if he'd asked to stay in that moment she probably would've said yes. The problem was he didn't want her to regret it later.

The chill of the night air seeped through his jacket, cooling his overheated skin. God, what had come over him? He hadn't even properly kissed the woman yet, and his body was on fire with need. He quickened his pace, heading through the Christmas tree grove to get to the spacious one-bedroom cabin he was staying in.

The full moon lit the pathway, and he wondered if he'd ever be so lucky as to show her the inside of his temporary quarters. The cabin was downright gorgeous with its open-beam ceilings, modern gray cabinets in the kitchenette, and walk-in shower with four shower heads. The place wasn't huge, but it was luxurious. And he'd like nothing better than to share it with Holly for an evening.

He'd just bounded up the porch stairs when he heard someone clear their throat. Spinning around, he spotted Zach sitting in one of the wooden chairs, hidden in the evening shadows.

"How was your date?" Zach asked, getting to his feet.

"Good once I got her away from flying golf balls." Rex slipped the key into the lock and opened the door wide for his friend. "How long have you been here?"

"Just a few minutes." Zach strode into the cabin and headed straight for the refrigerator, grabbing two beers. After handing one to Rex, he made himself comfortable on the leather couch. "So... looks like the love spell is working. What are you going to do when she falls for you?"

Rex let out a heavy sigh and moved to the fireplace, lighting the wood he'd already stacked earlier in the day. "She knows I'm leaving after New Year's. No one is falling for anyone."

"That's a lie," Zach said, but there wasn't any heat behind it. His tone was matter-of-fact as he watched his friend settle in the nearby leather armchair.

"You're right. It's a lie because I might be the one who's in trouble this time," he admitted. "She's nothing like anyone else I've dated."

"You mean she's nothing like Sara." Zach put his beer down and propped his elbows on his knees as he leaned forward to study Rex.

"This doesn't have anything to do with Sara," Rex said bitterly, wondering how far Zach was going to take this conversation. He had half a mind to stride over to the door, hold it open, and invite his friend to leave. Instead, he downed half his beer and hoped Zach would drop it.

"Sure it doesn't," Zach said with a humorless chuckle. "Whatever happened between you two, it's clear she messed you up something good. You haven't dated anyone seriously since."

"What's wrong with being single? You're single, too. I don't see you putting a ring on anyone's finger," Rex shot back.

"Nothing at all. You're just the commitment type. Bachelorhood doesn't really work for you," Zach said. His narrowed eyes were full of challenge, obviously waiting for Rex to argue with him so he could prove some sort of point. Rex didn't take the bait.

"How was *your* date?" Rex asked his friend. "Were there anymore wayward golf ball incidents?"

He laughed. "It was fine. And nope. Nobody else was assaulted by overzealous putting."

"Fine? That's it? I thought Ilsa was your dream girl? Fine isn't exactly what I was expecting." Rex put his empty beer bottle down on a side table and peered at his friend. "Did you choke or something? Usually you have plenty of dating game."

Zach placed a hand on his chest and opened his mouth in a shocked O, faking his offense. "How dare you accuse me of being off my game. My game was completely on point, if you must know. It was... I don't know. Ilsa didn't seem herself. There's something going on there, and I can't quite put my finger on it. I think dating isn't in the cards for us. We're better as friends."

"Seriously? You've been pining over her for years, dude. How long have you waited for your chance with her? Now that you're both on the same page, you're just gonna throw in the towel after one awkward date?" Rex asked.

"I have not been pining," Zach insisted. "More like admiring. I can still do that without dating her."

Rex shook his head. "You're an idiot. She was just nervous. Give her a break. That ugly face of yours the ladies seem to like so much probably left her tongue-tied."

Zach let out a bark of laughter. "Ilsa, tongue-tied? You've got to be kidding me. She has more sass in her pinky finger than all the women in this town combined. I have never seen her tongue-tied in my entire life. No way."

"You're overthinking this," Rex said. "You should just take her out again. Or does this retreat have something to do with Whitney?"

An emotionless mask suddenly replaced Zach's easy smile as he stared his friend in the eye. "We're not talking about Whitney."

"Why not? You brought up Sara," Rex challenged.

"That's different. It's been over ten years since your breakup with her. It's time you moved on." He crossed his arms over his chest and glared at Rex.

Rex laughed. "Right, because ten years is so much different than five."

"You haven't seen or talked to Sara in a decade. I see Whitney every week. It's not the same." There was a definite warning in his tone now.

"Fine." Rex threw his hands up in defeat. "You don't have to talk about her. But I'm starting to think that this has everything to do with Whitney considering how touchy you are about it."

Zach stood abruptly and moved to the door. "Thanks for the beer. I'll see you in the morning."

"Sure, man," Rex said as he also stood and walked over to his friend. After clasping him on the shoulder, he gave him a nod and added, "I really do think Ilsa's into you. Don't write her off so quickly."

He shrugged. "Maybe." His eyes narrowed again, and he said, "Be careful with Holly. She's been hurt before."

"We're just friends, Zach," Rex insisted.

"Sure. That's why when you look at her, your expression says you want to eat her for breakfast."

"It does not."

"Yes, it does, Rex," Zach said. "I've known you for fifteen years. You want her. I'm just asking you to be careful."

Rex didn't say anything. How could he? His friend was right and they both knew it.

CHAPTER 10

"You need to put me out of my misery," Ilsa said dramatically as she flopped down onto Holly's couch.

Holly shuffled in from her kitchen, her hands covered in cookie dough. She'd been making cookies when she heard Ilsa barge into the house and announce her presence. She'd woken up that day with her ankle as good as new and had been happily puttering around her house ever since she'd gotten home from the library. "What happened?"

Ilsa, who was covering her face with her hands, spread her fingers open and peeked at Holly. "I'm a complete idiot. There's no way Zach is going to take me out again."

Holly held up her dough covered hands. "Come into the kitchen and tell me all about it."

"Is there booze?" Ilsa whined.

"When isn't there booze?" Holly said with a chuckle.

Her overly dramatic friend hauled herself up off the couch. "There had better be something stronger than beer in there. I need some liquid courage if I'm ever going to talk to Zach again."

"Tequila or whiskey? Take your pick," Holly said, moving back behind her counter where she continued to roll out her peanut butter cookies.

Ilsa opened the liquor cabinet but didn't make a move to grab any of the bottles. After a moment, she closed it and went to the wine rack. "I better not go too crazy. Who knows what I'll do if I get too tipsy."

"Just don't drink the entire bottle yourself. Pour me a glass, will you?" Holly asked as she slid a tray into the oven. After setting the timer, she washed away the remaining dough and took the wine glass Ilsa held out to her. "All right. Spill. What happened after we left?"

"I was a complete moron. Can you believe I accidentally grabbed his crotch?" Her face turned bright red as she added, "And then I was so freaked out that I didn't let go right away. I just stood there, holding him, while he stared at my hand and asked if I was propositioning him."

"Oh, Ilsa." Holly choked out a laugh. "How did that happen?"

"I was reaching for his golf club when he twisted to face me and... I don't know. One minute I was teasing him about his putting swing and the next I was molesting him. I swear, I almost cast a spell to make it rain just so I'd have an excuse to get out of there."

"That would've been dramatic considering how much energy that takes," Holly said. Ilsa had the power. She was a water witch after all, but changing the actual weather was quite a feat. She'd have been laid out for days if she'd managed to open up the skies and make it rain.

"Right." She took a big gulp of her wine. "Instead, I released him and kept my hands to myself for the rest of the night. I didn't even put my arms around him when he kissed me goodnight."

"What did you do? Just stand there?" Holly tilted her head to the side, studying her friend.

"Yes. It was as if I was frozen. I was such a disaster the entire night that I fully expected him to bolt. Instead, he kissed me." She slumped, looking miserable.

"It's because he likes you, Ilsa. Can't you see that? The sexual tension between you two has been off the charts ever since that night you two danced at Vixen's a couple of weeks ago. Didn't you see the way he was looking at you last night? I swear he was undressing you with his eyes."

"No, he wasn't. You're just seeing things through lust-colored glasses. Ever since Rex came to town, you've been dying to rip his clothes off," she said.

Holly couldn't disagree with that last statement. There was no denying she was attracted to Rex Holiday. If he'd made a move last night, she had no doubt she'd have invited him to stay over. Her hormones were definitely in charge when he was around, her heart be damned. She knew she should protect herself and keep her distance, but she just didn't think she was that strong. "Maybe you're right about my lust-colored glasses, but I don't think so. You and Zach have amazing chemistry even if things are a little rocky."

"Whatever," she said, getting up and retrieving Sabrina the rabbit from her new habitat that Holly had picked up on the way home from work. "I'm just gonna play auntie to your rabbit and pretend Zach doesn't exist." She eyed her friend. "Now, tell me what happened with Rex."

"Nothing happened," Holly said, getting up to retrieve the cookies from the oven. After she inserted a second tray to bake, she turned her attention to the chocolate kisses that needed to be pressed into the tops of the hot cookies.

"Liar," Ilsa said. "You're blushing! Did you sleep with him? Oh my god. You did. You slept with him, didn't you?"

Holly rolled her eyes "No. Of course not. I barely know the guy."

"So." Ilsa moved around the counter and peered at Holly. "What did you do after you left the arcade?"

"He took me on a carriage ride to see the holiday lights. Nothing special." Holly quickened her pace, making sure she got a kiss pressed into each cookie before they cooled too much.

"That sounds pretty romantic to me," Ilsa said with a sigh. "It's too bad I didn't make that suggestion to Zach. I doubt I would've ended up assaulting him if we were both stationary."

"Seriously?" Holly gave her friend a side-eye glance. "Are you trying to say that if you were sharing a blanket you wouldn't have gotten handsy?" Chaste wasn't a word she'd use to describe her bestie. At least not when it came to men she'd fallen head over heels for. If she liked a guy, she had no problem getting physical.

"Are you calling me easy?" her friend asked in mock offense.

"No. You are anything but easy," Holly said with a laugh and wiped her hands on her Christmas apron. "You're actually very selective. But you're also usually the one to make the first move. And you didn't even have the chemistry with some of your past dating partners that you do with Zach. I honestly think it's only a matter of time before you two end up spending the night together."

"Nope. Never gonna happen," she insisted. "I'm too much of

a bumbling fool around him. I'm pretty sure I scared him off for good."

"I doubt that's true," Holly said and handed her a cookie.

She took a bite and let out a little moan of approval. "Holy hell, Hols. This is yummy."

"Thanks."

"Who are they for?" Ilsa asked.

Holly felt her face flush. "Rex. He mentioned something about them last night. I had the ingredients and the time, so I figured, why not?"

"Oh, honey," Ilsa said, giving Holly a sympathetic look. "You've got it bad, don't you? Please be careful with that one."

"Careful? Of what? He seems like the nicest guy on the planet. Look at how he helped me when I hurt my foot. Besides, he's one of Zach's best friends. Zach wouldn't be friends with a jerk."

"No. He wouldn't," Ilsa agreed. "But last night Zach mentioned that Rex hasn't had a long-term relationship in forever. He never sticks around long enough for a relationship to go anywhere. I just don't want you to get your heart broken."

"Wait, weren't you the one who told me it was time for me to have a little fun?" Holly demanded. Where was this coming from? Usually her friend was always trying to get Holly to loosen up and not be so serious. "Two days ago, you all but ordered me to sleep with Rex. Now you're telling me to be careful? Make up your mind already. Which is it? Stay away or throw myself at him?"

Ilsa let out a sigh. "I'm not telling you to stay away from him." She cuddled Sabrina in close to her chest and gave the bunny a kiss on the head. "It's just that I can see that you really like him. And even though we already knew he was leaving,

73

Zach's confirmed that he isn't relationship material even if you guys decided to try to give it a go long distance or whatever. I just don't want to see you hurt."

"Don't worry about me." Holly arranged the peanut butter cookies on a platter and set them in the middle of her breakfast table. "I'm not looking for a relationship. Just someone to take me to the ball and maybe kiss me at midnight on New Year's. Is that too much to ask?"

"No. Definitely not," Ilsa said, giving her friend a bright smile. "I'm sorry. I didn't mean to be a Grinch. Of course you should have some fun."

Holly nodded and moved back into the kitchen where she poured herself a cup of decaf coffee she'd brewed while working on the cookies. She understood what Ilsa was saying. If the shoe were on the other foot, she'd be warning her best friend about getting hurt, too. But what Ilsa didn't know was that Holly understood why Rex didn't stick around. After learning about his ex-fiancée, it was no surprise that he would have commitment issues.

Rex and Holly were fundamentally incompatible. She needed someone to stay, and he needed someone temporary. The only question was if she could be temporary just this once. She wasn't sure, but this time, she knew she wanted to try. Maybe it would be different if she knew they had an expiration date.

"Do you think I could have some of that?" Ilsa asked, nodding to Holly's cup of joe.

"Of course." Holly smiled warmly at her friend and handed her a mug of coffee with the special nondairy creamer she kept just for Ilsa.

"I love you. You know that, right?" Ilsa said.

"I do." Holly put her arm around her friend and pulled her in for a sideways hug. "I love you, too."

The pair were silent for a few moments until they heard a loud banging sound coming from somewhere in the front of the house.

"Are you putting in a pool finally?" Ilsa asked hopefully.

"In December? Seriously?"

Ilsa laughed. "Wishful thinking. But really, what's going on? Are you having work done on the property or something?"

Holly shook her head. "Nope. I guess we better go take a look. Maybe it's a road crew or something."

After Ilsa put Sabrina back in her bunny habitat, the pair made their way outside and down the driveway. As they rounded the corner near the old pumpkin patch clearing, Holly let out a gasp and clasped her hand over her mouth when she saw the large tent being erected.

"Um, Hols?" Ilsa asked. "What's this? Did you rent the place out for a wedding reception or something?"

"No. Not a wedding." She grinned as she spotted Rex directing one of the crew who were erecting the tent. "It's for my Hogwarts Christmas decorations."

Ilsa turned to stare at her. "Hogwarts?"

"You know, from the Harry Potter books. We're putting together the Great Hall at Christmas time." Holly waved at Rex and strode over to meet him.

"Hey! Look at you. You're walking on your own without a limp in sight. I assume you're pain free?" he said when she reached his side.

"Pain free." She demonstrated by lifting her right ankle and rotating it to prove she was cured. "Apparently my recovery is all thanks to you," she said.

"Healer Harrison gets some of the credit." He wrapped an

arm around her shoulder. "What do you think? I stopped in the party store and they had a cancellation today, so I booked it. I hope that's all right."

"Of course it's okay. Look at it!" The tent was almost fully erect. It was even tall and had a doomed ceiling, just like the hall in the Hogwarts castle. "Now I need to find an air witch."

"Already taken care of," he said with a wink and gestured to Lemon Pepperson, the owner of Christmas Grove Express. "She was at the party store and offered to help when she overheard me talking about the idea."

Holly eyed her. "For a fee I imagine." Lemon Pepperson didn't do much of anything without getting paid. Hustle was the woman's middle name.

"That's the best part. She's doing it for a trade," Rex said as he waved Lemon over.

"Trade for what?" It wasn't as if Holly had much of anything other than berries, but they were out of season and all she had were a few dozen bags in the freezer.

"Thank you!" Lemon gushed as she hurried over to them. "You have no idea what a huge relief this is."

Holly blinked at her. "What's a huge relief?"

"Oh, my goodness, that you're taking over the duties to collect the toys for the toy drive. Between being down a couple of employees and having to make delivery runs and dealing with all the local businesses, I've been losing my mind. This is such a load off."

Holly's eyebrows shot up as she widened her eyes at Rex. She didn't have time to deal with collecting the toys. How was she going to manage when she had to work at the library all day? The reason Lemon usually collected them was because someone was in her storefront all the time.

"Don't worry," Rex said, slipping his arm around her waist. "I've got a plan."

"Rex, I can't be the point person. There aren't enough hours in the day." Panic was starting to set in as she frantically started to mentally rearrange her schedule to deal with collections.

"Whoa, calm down there, Holly. I'm going to be the point person," Rex said.

"You? Really?" She stared at him, trying to figure out why he'd take on such a huge task for Christmas Grove. "Do you have any idea how much work that will be?"

"I do," he said with a chuckle. "Don't worry about it. My schedule is flexible. But I was hoping we could make the Great Hall the collection point. I think it would help with donations."

Holly stared up at him in awe. How was it possible this guy was so amazing? And why the hell had Sara treated him so horribly? Tears stung her eyes as she nodded and said, "Of course we can. I think that's a wonderful idea."

"Good." His smile grew and he opened his arms, inviting a hug.

Holly didn't even think twice. She walked right into his embrace and held on tight, loving every moment she was in his arms.

CHAPTER 11

Two hours later, the Great Hall was up, and faux stone walls had been fixed to both the inside and the outside of the tent to make it resemble something out of a Harry Potter movie. Plans were made to bring in long wooden tables and nearly a dozen Christmas trees the next day, and Lemon promised to stop by after work to spell the candles.

"By tomorrow night, the Hogwarts experience will be in full effect," Rex said as he, Holly, and Ilsa made their way back into the house. He glanced at Holly, loving the way her red hair spilled down her back in soft waves. She was wearing a wool fitted dress that hugged all of her curves and black leather boots. Everything about her screamed sophistication, and he couldn't help but wonder what she was wearing underneath her clothes. His insides fluttered with anticipation, but he shook his head slightly, trying to force himself back into the moment. What had he been talking about? Right. Hogwarts. "Didn't you say you have a sorting hat? We'll need to remember to have Lemon spell it, too."

"Can she do that?" Ilsa asked. "I know she can make it move, but can she make it talk, too?"

"I think so. She's pretty powerful," Holly said, not bothering to hide her excitement as her eyes danced and she bounced on the balls of her feet. "It'll probably have to be redone a few times before the season is over. We'll just have to make sure we use it only during events or something."

"I just hope I'm not a Slytherin," Rex said with a laugh. He'd been as much of a Harry Potter freak as the next kid back in high school, and he loved helping Holly set up the Christmas version of the Great Hall.

"You?" Ilsa scoffed. "No way. I bet you're a Hufflepuff."

He blinked at her. "Is that supposed to be an insult?" he asked. "Because if it is, I'm not bothered. Hufflepuffs are extremely loyal. That's one of my best qualities if I do say so myself."

A laugh bubbled out of Holly's parted lips. "I like the Puffs. And as much as I want to be a Gryffindor, I'm probably more of a Ravenclaw. Librarian blood."

"Yeah. You're definitely a Ravenclaw," Ilsa said.

Holly led the way into her kitchen and was about to start looking through her cabinets for something to make for dinner when Rex's arms came around her. He covered her hands with his and said, "Oh, no you don't. I'm making dinner, remember? A deal's a deal."

"On that note... time to go!" Ilsa called as she spun on her heel and started making tracks toward the front of the house.

"Ilsa, wait!" Holly cried and extracted herself from Rex's arms, much to his disappointment. He liked Ilsa plenty, but that didn't mean he wanted to share his limited time with Holly with her. As far as he was concerned, she was doing them a favor by making herself scarce.

While Holly went to talk to Ilsa, Rex got to work in the kitchen. After a quick inventory, he opted for pesto and sundried tomato chicken to be served over parmesan pasta. By the time Holly made it back into the kitchen, he already had a glass of white wine waiting for her.

"Ilsa had to get home. She said something about cleaning her andirons. Whatever that means," Holly said.

Rex snickered. "It's a *When Harry Met Sally* reference. It means she made up an excuse to get out of here. Can't say I'm unhappy about that, though. I've been looking forward to a quiet dinner with you all day."

"You have?" she asked, her eyes going soft as she gazed at him.

"Definitely. Now take a drink of the wine and let me know what you think."

She tipped the glass to her lips and then nodded in appreciation. "This one is my favorite."

"Me too," he said as he watched her, only he wasn't talking about the wine. He was referring to the gorgeous creature in front of him. He wished he'd had time to light a few candles, maybe put some romantic music on. Instead, they were standing under the harsh lighting of the kitchen as they listened to the rabbit chew on some baby carrots he'd tucked into her cage, and he'd decided he wouldn't have it any other way.

"After we eat, we really need to finish those Christmas cookies," she said.

"You're on." Rex busied himself finishing their dinner while Holly worked on rolling out the dough and using her cookie cutters to turn the cookies into snowmen, Christmas trees, and snowflakes. Once they were in the oven, she set the table while Rex plated the food. It wasn't long before the oven timer went off and the smell of fresh baked cookies filled the air.

"Those smell delicious," Rex said, plating their dinner.

"Not as delicious as your pesto chicken," she said.

Rex set a plate of chicken and pasta in front of her where she sat at the table and then took the seat next to her.

Her eyes widened as she stared at the plate. "This looks and smells amazing."

"I hope it lives up to expectation," he said and forked a mouthful of pasta.

She did the same and let out a little noise of appreciation. "Were you a chef in another life?"

"Maybe. But in this one I'm just an amateur." He dug into his dinner, enjoying watching her eat the meal he'd created. Judging by the way she used a roll to sop up every last bit of sauce on her plate, she wasn't worried about appearing dainty. And he appreciated her healthy appetite. Food was one of his passions, and he loved sharing it with someone.

Once her plate was wiped clean, she pushed it aside and smiled at him. "That was wonderful. I'm afraid if you keep this up you're going to spoil me."

"That's exactly what I intend to do over the next four weeks," he said as he got up and deposited their dishes in the sink. On his way back to the table, he brought the cooled Christmas cookies and decorations Holly had already set out over to the table.

Once he was seated, he held the wine bottle up. "Refill?"

"Yes," she breathed, watching him with a pleased smile on her face. "You weren't kidding about spoiling me, were you?"

"Holly, I'm one hundred percent serious. You're kind, generous, gorgeous, and I can't think of anyone else I would rather spend my time with here in Christmas Grove over the next weeks."

"Good. Cause I feel the same way about you." She pointed to the covered platter she'd left in the middle of the table. "Those are for you."

"You made me something?" he asked, already reaching for the platter. When he opened it and spotted the peanut butter and chocolate kiss cookies, his heart melted. She'd been paying attention when he said he had a craving for them. "Thank you." He leaned over and brushed the lightest of kisses over her cheek. He didn't miss the way her eyes closed or the tiny shudder that ran through her body. His own body answered with a shiver of desire, and he had to swallow a groan. He cleared his throat. "These look amazing."

"Try one," she urged.

Rex hadn't needed the encouragement. He was already salivating over the cookies. After handing her one, he bit into the soft cookie and didn't hold back his sounds of pleasure. "Damn, Holly. This might be the best peanut butter cookie I've ever had." He snatched a couple more, already mentally adding a couple of miles to his morning run. "Did you add some secret ingredient to hook your victims or something?"

"Or something." Her grin was wide as she added, "You'll need to make it to that baking class to find out."

That wasn't going to be a problem. He would've already called to reserve a spot, but since she mentioned he could use her station, there was no way he was going to pass up that opportunity. "Good. I can't wait to get my baking on."

She eyed him with something that looked a lot like suspicion, but when she blinked, the suspicion was gone and all that was left was a cheerful woman, ready to decorate the last of the Christmas cookies. She handed him a pastry bag filled with green icing. "Okay. You Ready for your first lesson?"

"More than ready," he said, waiting to see what she wanted him to do.

She stood and grabbed her own pastry bag filled with white icing. "It's pretty easy. Just pipe an outline of icing on the cookie like this." She outlined the snowflake in white. "Then fill it in." After covering the cookie in white icing, she used a toothpick to smooth it out. "After it settles, you can add whatever sprinkles you want."

"Looks straightforward enough," he said and got to work.

An hour later, all the cookies were decorated with varying degrees of success, and when Holly glanced up at Rex, she burst out laughing.

"What is it?" he asked, pushing his hair back and out of his eyes.

She laughed harder.

"Holly?" Rex walked over to her and started to reach for her hips, ready to draw her closer, but she jumped back.

"Your hands!" She laughed and held her own up, keeping him at bay. "You need to wipe them off before you touch me, otherwise, I'll probably look like a reject from the beauty counter, too."

"Oh, hell," he said, gingerly touching his face. "Do I have it all over?"

She nodded, still snorting with laughter. "I'd try to wipe it off, but it might be a bigger job than that.

"I'll be right back." Rex disappeared into the downstairs bathroom and let out a groan when he saw his reflection in the mirror. She hadn't been exaggerating. There was a rainbow of red, green, and white icing on the left side of his face. How had he not noticed he was smearing it all over? Probably because he was too busy watching Holly. Her movements were so sure and smooth, so graceful. Sometime in the last hour, he'd decided he could be happy watching her for the rest of his days. She had a quality about her that put him at ease and made him feel content. It wasn't something he was used to.

After he washed up, he returned to the kitchen to find Holly cleaning up the dinner dishes. He stepped right in, helping put away the cookie supplies and drying dishes she wasn't willing to put in the dishwasher. It was all so domestic, and yet, a welcome change in his life. Maybe it was because he didn't lead the most stable life, always moving and never putting down roots. But everything about the time they spent together that night filled all of Rex's empty spaces, and he knew he didn't want it to end.

"Rex?" Holly asked as she dried her hands on a hand towel.

"Yeah?" He leaned against the counter and stared at her full lips, the desire to kiss her making him unable to focus on anything else.

"There's a Christmas ball every year in the town square. I was wondering if you planned on going," she asked, her voice huskier than normal.

"A Christmas ball?" he asked, not quite processing her question.

"Yes. It's a formal event where money is raised for charity." She moved in and placed her hands on his hips. "Do you have a date?"

His lips curved into a ghost of a smile. "No. Do you?"

She shook her head. "But I'm looking for one."

"I think your search is over, Ms. Reineer." Then he closed the distance and kissed her with everything he had.

CHAPTER 12

*T*he next day as Holly worked the checkout counter at the town library, she could still feel the tingle of Rex's kiss on her lips. That kiss had been hot. Smokin' hot if she was honest. She couldn't remember ever being kissed like that before, and she'd been two seconds away from leading him upstairs to her bedroom when he'd broken the kiss and hastily said goodnight.

The abrupt loss had left her feeling slightly rejected. He'd wanted her. There was no doubt about that. She just didn't understand why he kept running away the moment they started to get physical. What was he afraid of? She let out a long sigh and sat back in her chair.

"Why the long face?" a familiar high-pitched voice asked.

Holly jerked her head up and smiled at Lily Paddington, her favorite patron, and her son, Evan. The sweet blonde was holding a stack of kid's books.

"Who do I need to—" She glanced down at Evan and shrugged as she cleared her throat. "I mean, what's the trouble, love?"

Holly stood and took the books from Lily as she smiled at her. "It's nothing. Just trying to work something out."

"Does it have to do with your Christmas decorations? I hear y'all are putting on quite a show." She once again glanced down at her son and then pressed a finger to her lips, indicating to Holly not to reveal the details.

Holly nodded, understanding completely. "Oh, no. The decorations should be done later this afternoon. You two should come by and sign up for the Christmas party."

Lily's expression darkened. "Party?"

"Kid's party. Everything is taken care of. You just need to sign up so we have an accurate count." Holly knew Lily struggled with her budget, and she didn't want to embarrass her, but she also wanted to make sure her sweet son got something on his list from Santa. "Come by any time before the Christmas Ball to sign up. The family party is a few days after."

"Okay. We'll try." Lily gave her a grateful smile and took the books Holly handed back to her.

Holly leaned down so that she was eye level with Evan. "Hey, sweetie."

"Hi," he said with a shy smile.

"Those are some great choices you picked out. Enjoy them and let me know what you think when you come in next week, okay?"

"Okay," he said, giving her a bright smile.

Holly grinned and put her fist out to him.

The little boy bumped her fist with his and let out a loud laugh.

"Thank you, Holly," Lily said again. Her eyes were bright and her smile soft as she glanced down at Evan. "Thanks for always making this a place he wants to visit."

"Always," Holly said and waved as they made their way out of the library. When they were gone, she smiled to herself and said, "That, right there. That's what makes it all worth it."

"Makes what all worth it?" a familiar voice asked.

She glanced up to find Rex striding toward her, a Christmas themed lunch box in one hand. "The toy drive. Lily Paddington and her little boy are making it okay, but extras... Christmas isn't in the budget."

"You mean the pretty blonde and her little mini me?" he asked curiously as he handed her the lunch box.

"They come in every week. Evan loves books," Holly said, eyeing the lunch box.

"Really. Do you think they've read Harry Potter yet?" He moved closer to the desk and leaned over, brushing his lips over her cheek.

"Just the first one. Lily's read it to him. She's trying to draw it out so they can savor them together."

He nodded. "Excellent. Can't wait to see what he thinks of the Great Hall."

"Heck, I can't wait to see the Great Hall." She held the lunch box up. "What's in here?"

"I thought you might like to try my goat cheese raviolis." He gave her a self-satisfied smile.

"You seriously made goat cheese raviolis?" she asked, her eyes wide with both shock and appreciation.

He laughed. "No. They are leftovers from lunch at Pine Needles. I couldn't eat them all and thought you might want to try them."

Her mouth watered just thinking about it. "These are my absolute favorite. Thank you!"

"I know. Ellie might have mentioned it." He winked at her, referring to the restaurant owner. "Now, what time do you get off? I want to make sure everything is ready before you get home."

"What's everything?" she asked, not really paying attention. She was too busy opening the lunch box and pulling out a plastic container full of her favorite meal ever.

"The Christmas decorations of course. And dinner. I'm just trying to work out my timing." He gave her a half-shrug as if all of this was completely normal.

"Rex?" she asked, tilting her head to the side to study him.

"Yeah?" He had a look of mock innocence.

"What are you up to?" she demanded. "Why are you putting so much energy into this?" *Into me*, she wanted to ask but didn't.

"Because I love Christmas and I love to cook. What more could I ask for? My two favorite things combined with a theme from the best books of all time and the prettiest girl in town to share it all with... What's not to love?"

She shook her head, hardly able to believe that he had that much time and energy to devote to her, the toy drive, and her fantastical whims of recreating part of the Hogwarts castle. "Don't you have to work, ever?"

"Sure." He nodded. "I got all of my work done for Zach this morning. This afternoon and evening are all yours, Holly. Be there or be square," he said with a cheesy grin.

"I'll be there," she said, unable to hide the grin claiming her own lips. Rex Holiday wasn't the kind of man she was used to, but she suspected she could adjust really quickly.

He leaned across the counter, and this time his lips brushed hers, lingering for just a moment as if to make promises of what was to come. She wanted to tell her boss she was heading home for the day, that she'd come in early to put away the books that had come in. Instead, she found herself standing there like a complete idiot, drooling over the gorgeous man who'd not only made her Hogwarts Christmas come to life but also figured out her favorite dish from Pine Needles. He was too good to be true. Way, *way* too good to be true.

She was already becoming spoiled. What was she going to do when he finally left town? She'd be heartbroken. There was no doubt about it. But still, all of their interactions made it one hundred percent worth it. Whatever Rex Holiday had to give, she'd take it. She had no choice really. He'd already pulled her into the deep end.

The only question was, would she swim or sink?

She was going to do her damnedest to swim, but she couldn't deny the appeal of being pulled under his spell. He flipped all of her switches, and that was headier than she cared to admit.

"See you in a few hours," Rex said just before he disappeared out of the library.

"Looks like he's going to be seeing a lot of you," Josie, her boss, teased. "Whoa! That chemistry. I think you gave me a hot flash." She fanned herself with a sheet of paper.

Yeah. That chemistry. It was going to get her into some real trouble. Only now the problem was that she just didn't think she cared anymore what happened after Rex left town. She was too far gone not to succumb to temptation. She'd deal with the fallout in January.

HOLLY PULLED into her long driveway and drove past a line of cars parked off to the side. When she reached the Great Hall tent, she spotted a group of kids and their parents staring wide-eyed at the magical space. A huge grin claimed her lips, and nothing made her happier than seeing all of the little faces alight with wonder.

After parking her car in the front of her Victorian, she made her way back down to the tent just in time to see a line of kids get sorted by the magical hat. It had been spelled to move, it's folds appearing to be talking while a PA system called out the difference houses. It didn't take her long to realize the recording was on a loop.

"Hey there, handsome," Holly said, stopping next to Rex, who was busy setting up a collection bin. "This is amazing. Who put the word out?"

He glanced up and smiled at her. "Lemon. After she spelled the candles, I think she told everyone she ran into that they could drop off the toys for the toy drive here. She might be just a tiny bit excited about handing off that task."

Holly snorted. "I'm sure." She scanned the area near the front of the Great Hall. He'd found a large plastic receptacle for the toys, and there was a folding table with poster board and markers lying on top of it. "Want me to do the donation sign?"

"Would you?" Relief washed over him as his face relaxed, and he let out an exaggerated breath. "My handwriting is crap."

"You appear to have done everything else. It's the least I can do." She leaned over and gave him a kiss on his cheek before tucking behind the table and getting to work.

Once she had the sign ready to go, complete with drawings of witches' hats, black cats, wands, and candles, she called Rex over. "Can you help me hang this?"

"It looks great, Hols," he said, making her puff up with pride.

It was silly. All she'd done was draw a few cute Halloween decorations on the sign, but his praise lit her up. And by the time they had the sign affixed to the tent wall, his nearness was making her want to drag him back to her house just to get him alone. How many days did they have before he left to go back east? Not nearly enough and she was starting to feel greedy for them.

"Holly!" a woman exclaimed.

She turned her attention to the woman and spotted none other than her library patron, Lily, and her son Evan moving quickly toward her. Both had huge grins on their faces while their eyes were bright with wonder. "Hey, Lily, Evan. I'm glad you could make it."

"This is fantastic," Lily gushed as she waved a hand around and then pointed to the giant Christmas tree at the front of the hall. "It's the most perfect tree I've ever seen. Look at the sweet little red birds perched in the limbs. Not to mention the animated owls in the rafters. The details… They are just incredible."

Holly squinted up at the rafters and laughed. She hadn't even noticed the owls. The one closest to the giant tree and where the kids were being sorted was a snowy white owl that look a lot like a certain favorite one of Harry's. She turned and grinned at Rex. "You thought of everything."

He shrugged one shoulder as if to say it was no big deal and then winked at her. Her insides turned to mush, and it was as if a spell had been cast over her. One that made her want to wrap her arms around him and never let him go. It could have been the love spell working its magic, but she didn't think so. What she was feeling had everything to do with the man who'd walked into her life and made her smile everyday just by being himself.

"Evan brought something for the toy drive," Lily said. She crouched down beside the boy and whispered in his ear.

Evan produced a stuffed gray wolf that Holly recognized as his favorite toy. She cut her gaze to Lily and furrowed her brow in question. "That's not Benji, is it?"

Lily nodded as her eyes misted. "It is. Evan wants him to watch over someone else who might need him."

Holly's heart swelled and nearly cracked in two as she gently took the stuffed wolf from Evan. The boy lifted his trembling chin and gave her a decisive nod as if answering the question she hadn't yet asked. *Was he sure he wanted to do this?*

"Benji is a good wolf," Evan said. "He'll make someone who needs him very happy." The boy took one last look at the wolf and then turned and ran out of the hall.

"Oh, Lily. Are you sure you want to let him do this?" Holly asked, clutching the stuffed wolf to her chest. "Isn't Benji his favorite?"

Lily nodded. "He is, but Evan insisted when he heard about the toy drive. We don't…" She cleared her throat. "Um, there's not a lot left over in the budget for new stuff, so Evan picked out one of his toys. I never expected him to choose Benji, but he did. And he's adamant that he wants someone to have him."

"I just…" Holly looked at Rex and then back at Lily. "I don't understand. Won't Evan miss him?"

A single tear ran down Lily's cheek. "Yes, he will. But he also knows what it's like to not have a lot. He wants to do his part to help. It's important to him, so I can't exactly tell him he can't."

Oh, hell. Holly blinked back her tears. She clutched the wolf to her chest and nodded. "Okay. We'll find him a great home."

"I know you will." She gave Holly a watery smile, thanked her again for the wonderful experience of letting Evan live out a childhood fantasy, and then left to collect her son.

Holly collapsed into a folding chair and let out a long breath.

"That was something else," Rex said, still watching as Lily caught up to her son.

"It all but tore my heart out," Holly said, her voice catching on a tiny sob.

Rex turned to look at her and then slipped behind the table to put his hands on her shoulders. As he gently rubbed her muscles, he said, "It looks like Lily is signing Evan up for the gifting party. How is that going to work? Are the kids sponsored individually or are toys just given out at random?"

"Individually. Anonymous angels pick who they want to sponsor. If there is anyone left over, we'll do our best to find them angels. If we run out of volunteers, then the ball committee takes them on and gets them something special from their list."

"I'd like to be Evan's sponsor," Rex said.

Holly's heart felt as if it was going to explode. Of course he did. So did she. The sweet boy was so selfless she wanted to make sure he had the best Christmas ever. "Only if I can help."

Rex leaned down and kissed her on the top of her head. "I wouldn't have it any other way."

CHAPTER 13

*J*t was almost eight in the evening by the time the crowds finally left the Great Hall. Parents and kids alike were delighted by the display. Many had already shown up with toys for the toy drive and to ogle the magical space. Finally, Rex had taken matters into his own hands and told them they were welcome to enjoy the decorations but that he and Holly were turning in for the evening. Otherwise, he was afraid he and Holly would never get dinner. They couldn't survive another three weeks of nonstop visitors if they didn't set some personal boundaries. Some limits had to be in place.

"My feet are killing me," Holly said as she opened the front door of her Victorian and waved him in. "I had no idea the Hall would be so successful."

Rex let out a bark of laughter as he headed for her kitchen. He heard her footsteps behind him as he said, "We were so naïve."

"It won't be like that all the way up to Christmas, will it?" Holly asked, kicking her shoes off. She flopped onto the couch and started rubbing her sore ankle.

"I thought your ankle had healed," Rex said, moving to sit on the coffee table in front of her.

"It did, but after milling around the tent for a few hours, it's started to ache," she said, giving him a tired smile.

"Let me do that." Rex sat across from her on her coffee table and took her foot into his capable hands. The moment his fingers touched her bare skin, he let that tiny spark of magic fly and was gratified to hear her sigh in relief.

"Damn, you're good at that." She sank back into the cushions and closed her eyes, a tiny satisfied smile claiming her lips.

He was dying to lean in and kiss her, but he kept to his spot on the table, gently massaging her foot instead. If he did kiss her, he wasn't sure he could stop. And he still had to make her dinner. After a few minutes, Holly looked as if he'd massaged all the tension right out of her. Rex chuckled and ran his hands firmly over her calf before releasing her and getting to his feet. "I need to get into the kitchen and get started on dinner."

Holly opened one eye and peered at him and then the clock on the wall. "How about takeout?"

He shook his head. "Nah. I've got this. You just relax. I'll have something ready to go before the food could get here anyway."

"You really don't have to do all of this you know," Holly said, her gaze moving to his mouth.

Rex's body tensed with pure desire. There was no mistaking what she was thinking in that moment. His body screamed for him to move back to the couch, to sit next to her and take her in his arms. But before he could move, his stomach rumbled, filling the silence between them. Son of a...

Holly chuckled and pushed herself up off the couch. "Let me help at least."

"No argument here." He placed his hand on the small of her back, loving just having her near. A faint cookie scent filled his senses, and he wondered if she always smelled like a bakery. Or was it just at Christmas? He was dying to find out, except once New Year's came around... He shook his head. That was one thing he wasn't going to let himself think about. He was here now. That was all that mattered.

Once they were in the kitchen, Rex got busy making a simple tomato and basil pasta dish while Holly put together a salad. After they ate, they stood side by side at her sink, cleaning up as if they'd been doing dishes together for years. It struck Rex that he couldn't ever remember feeling as comfortable with anyone he'd ever dated before, not even Sara.

"You're staring at me," she said, glancing over at him with an amused expression on her face. "Do I have tomato sauce on my chin or something?"

"No." But she did have some in the corner of her mouth, and he didn't hesitate to lean in and kiss her there. His tongue came out and licked the spot and then trailed along her lower lip.

She let out a tiny breath as she opened her mouth for him.

In the next moment, he had his arms around her and was pressing her against the counter as he kissed her with everything he had.

Holly melted into him, her hands moving to wrap around his neck.

Damn, she felt good, even better than he'd imagined, and he vaguely wondered if he'd have the will to let her go.

Not yet, his brain practically shouted at him, as if there was any way he was ready to release her. He tilted his head to the side, kissing her deeper. And when she let out a little moan of approval, his body went taut with pure desire.

"Holly," he murmured between kisses.

"Yes," she said and leaned into him, silently demanding more.

"If we don't stop soon, you're going to have a hell of a time getting me out of here." All of his nerve endings were sparking with desire. It had been a long time since he'd been with anyone and even longer since he'd wanted anyone as much as he wanted her.

"No one is asking you to leave," she breathed.

It was Rex's turn to let out an involuntary moan. He dipped his head, giving her a slow, hungry kiss. When he finally pulled away, he whispered, "Are you sure?"

"More than sure," she said, gazing up into his eyes with a hunger that told him everything he needed to know.

Rex took her by the hand and after a gentle tug, he led her through the house, up the stairs, and into her elegant bedroom. He barely glanced at the four-poster bed that was covered with an over-abundance of white linens and pillows. All he could see was Holly and her flushed face and kiss-swollen lips. She was gorgeous in every way and, at the moment, completely his.

Holly pressed her palms to his chest and glanced down for just a moment before looking back up at him, her lower lip caught between her teeth.

His heart plummeted into his gut. "Are you having second thoughts?"

"What?" she gasped out. Then she shook her head, making her red locks fan out behind her. "No. Not at all. I was just..." She let out a nervous chuckle. "It's just that I have this rule, and it might seem obvious, but I have to say it to be sure."

He raised his eyebrows, wondering where the heck this was going. Because nothing was obvious to him. Nothing other than he had her in her bedroom and the only thing he could think about was getting her naked. "What rule is that?"

"I don't do one-night stands." Her voice was so low he wasn't sure he heard her correctly.

"No one-night stands?" he asked.

"Right." She squared her shoulders and stared him in the eye. "I don't just hookup with people for a night. It's not my nature." She glanced away again, but quickly returned her gaze to his as if forcing herself to finish this conversation. "We both know you're leaving next month. And I accept that. But I need to know that if you stay over tonight that this isn't just a one-time thing and that you're not sleeping with anyone else."

He couldn't help the huge grin that spread across his face. Had she really just told him that she expected there to be a repeat of their night together? As if he'd ever say no to that. "You got it, Holly. I'd like nothing more than to spend the next few weeks getting to know every inch of your body. And what you said about sleeping with anyone else… That's not going to be an issue." He placed his hands on her slender hips and ran them up and down her sides. "I've always been a big fan of monogamy. And the same goes for you. I'm the only one who gets to touch all of this creamy skin."

"No argument here," she said as her hands slipped under his shirt, caressing his abs.

"Holly," he groaned, loving the gentle touch of her fingers.

"Yes?" Her tone was light and teasing as she slipped one hand down, this time grabbing hold of his butt.

"You're going to drive me crazy, aren't you?" he asked.

"Yes." She pressed her body against his and lifted up onto her tiptoes to whisper into his ear, "And I'm going to love every moment of it."

A zing of anticipation lit him up as he reached for her

again. But she put her hand out, stopping him, and held one finger up as if to say, *give me a minute.*

Rex stepped back, hating that his hands were no longer full of her gorgeous body. But even as he formed the thought in his head, Holly stalked toward him, already pulling her T-shirt over her head, leaving her in a gorgeous black lace bra that showed off every inch of her cleavage.

"Damn, Hols," he said quietly as he ran his fingertips over the swell of one of her breasts.

"You're so freakin' gorgeous. I can't believe my luck."

"Believe it, Rex," she demanded softly, reaching for his shirt and making quick work of the T-shirt he'd thrown on earlier in the day. And then they were skin to skin, heart to heart, and the rest of the world disappeared as they got lost in each other.

CHAPTER 14

*H*olly woke the next morning snuggled in Rex's arms, her head resting on his shoulder. When they'd finally gone to sleep the night before, she'd been prepared to feel slightly awkward about waking up naked in her bed with a man she'd only met a week before, but the only thing she felt was contentment. Being in Rex's arms was like coming home.

That thought should've scared her, but it didn't. Everything about being with Rex, even if it was only for a month, felt exactly right, and she had no desire to change anything. This was one thing she wasn't going to deprive herself of just because she was scared about how she'd feel when he walked back out of her life. She already knew she was going to be heartbroken, but she just didn't care. Not right then. Holly wouldn't have traded her time with the gorgeous man beneath her for anything in the world. The only thing left to do was enjoy him.

She rolled slightly into Rex and gave him a soft kiss on his shoulder.

"Hmm," he mumbled sleepily, tightening his grip on her shoulder.

"Good morning," she whispered.

"Yes, it is," he said, his voice full of sleep. "The only thing that would make it better is if you didn't need to go into work today."

She chuckled. "Don't *you* have work today, too?"

"Eh, probably." He hugged her close and pressed a kiss to her head. "But Zach is easily managed."

"I bet." She shook her head and rolled her eyes. "Must be nice to work for your best friend."

"It has its perks," he said and then threw the covers off of them.

"Hey!" she cried, scrambling to pull the blanket back over them. "It's cold. Don't do that again if you want a repeat of last night."

He turned his gorgeous blue eyes to her and raised one eyebrow, looking so sexy she almost forgot why she was irritated. Almost, but not quite as she shivered beneath the blanket.

"Repeat, huh," he said, his voice rough and so sexy her skin suddenly heated. Rex reached for her and tucked her in tightly to his warm body. "Was that an invitation?"

"I thought you had to get to work," she said, running a hand down his muscled back. She'd spent most of the night before reveling in the firmness of his body. It had been so long since she'd had anyone in her bed and never anyone she enjoyed more than Rex Holiday. Letting him leave to get to work was going to be a major challenge.

"Zach can wait." His lips came down on hers as she wrapped herself around him and got lost in everything he had to offer.

Forty-five minutes later, Holly walked Rex to her front door, handed him a travel mug of coffee, and kissed him lightly on the lips. "Dinner tonight?"

"Absolutely." He cupped the back of her head and pulled her in closer. "That little kiss isn't going to hold me over until five."

She laughed and melted into him, giving him the heated kiss he craved. When they pulled apart, they were both breathing a little bit too hard.

"Get a room!" Ilsa called from the bottom of the porch stairs.

Holly glanced around Rex at her best friend. She was dressed in jeans, knee-high boots, and a red sweater with a furry scarf covering her neck. "How long have you been there?"

"Long enough to need a cold shower." She fanned herself and grinned knowingly at them.

Holly rolled her eyes and gave her attention to Rex again. "Thanks for... everything." She swallowed, feeling her face heat.

He chuckled. "Right back at you, Hols. See you tonight." He winked, kissed her cheek, and finally let her go. As he strode past Ilsa, he grinned at her. "Have a good day."

"Oh, I will. But something tells me it's not going to be nearly as good as yours. Not all of us get to wake up naked next to—"

"Ilsa!" Holly cut her off and laughed. "Stop."

Ilsa shrugged and strode up onto the porch. "What? I'm just envious, that's all."

Holly rolled her eyes and then smiled at Rex one more time as he chuckled and disappeared around the side of her house as he made his way toward Zach's Christmas tree farm.

"Spill it. All of it," Ilsa demanded as she tugged Holly back into the large Victorian.

Holly shivered and wrapped her arms around herself, cursing that she'd forgotten to close the door, causing the December air to waft in.

"I need cookies for this." Ilsa glided into the kitchen, flipped on the space heater in the corner, and made herself at home as she raided the cookie jar and then poured herself a cup of coffee. "So," she said, letting her gaze travel the length of Holly's body. "You're supposed to be leaving for work in twenty minutes, but it looks like you might be naked under that robe."

"I don't have to be there until eleven," Holly muttered and opened the refrigerator to search out ingredients for an omelet. The activities from the night before had left her ravenous. Cookies weren't going to cut it.

"Called in late, did you?" Ilsa asked with a chuckle and continued to needle Holly. "That's unusual for you."

"So is having a guy stay over, but here we are," Holly said, retrieving the skillet from the cabinet next to the stove.

"Every girl deserves a little fun once in a while," Ilsa said, but her teasing tone had morphed into a serious one as she studied her friend.

Holly swallowed a groan. While Ilsa was saying the right things, her expression said something completely different. "Don't give me the 'be careful' speech again, all right? Last night…" Holly pressed her hand to her heart and took in a deep breath. "It was something I've never experienced before."

"You mean you let him go where no other man has gone before?" Ilsa's eyes danced with mischief, making Holly laugh.

"No, perv. I mean I've never felt like that before. So cared for, cherished even." Holly knew she sounded like a lovesick teenager, but she didn't care. Her time with Rex had been nothing short of magical. And not in a love potion magical way. It had been the magic of human connection and two souls who were right where they were supposed to be in that moment.

"Oh, honey." Ilsa had a pained look on her face, but then she sucked in her own breath and forced a smile. "I won't give you the speech again. You know my concerns."

"I do. To be honest, I have them, too, but it's also true that I'm helpless to stay away from him. So here we are. I've got about three or so weeks to enjoy that gorgeous man, and then it's back to bingo night at the senior's hall."

"You've never played bingo at the senior's hall," Ilsa said, rolling her eyes.

"No, but I might take it up." She smiled. "Or maybe I'll have to join the polar bear club. That will cool any lingering feelings for Rex once he's gone."

Ilsa studied her without saying anything for a moment. It was clear she disagreed that jumping into a freezing lake would do anything other than give Holly a mild case of frostbite, but she kept her opinion to herself this time. "Okay, now that we have that out of the way... How was he?"

Holly felt her face burn, and she shook her head, returning to her eggs to finish up the omelet. "We're not rating Rex's skill in the bedroom."

"Judging by the way you two were plastered together this morning, I'd say way above average. On a scale of one to ten, what do you say? Eight? Nine?"

Ten, Holly thought. *A solid ten*. But she just smiled to herself and added some bacon to her omelet. A girl needed a little extra protein after being up half the night. "Need breakfast?"

"Awe, what kind of bestie are you if you aren't even going

to dish about your night in the sack with the hottie from out of town?"

"A modest one who isn't going to be bullied by you," Holly said, careful to keep her tone light. She knew Ilsa was just teasing her, but Holly was ready for the conversation to be over. "But feel free to tell me all about what you'll do with Zach if you two ever get on the same page dating-wise."

Ilsa clapped her hands together. "I forgot to tell you why I came by this morning."

Holly glanced back at her friend, noting that she'd tied her long dark hair up into a haphazard bun. It was a sign Ilsa was settling in for some serious girl talk. Holly glanced at the clock, wondering why Ilsa wasn't at work. She managed a gift shop in town that Mrs. Pottson's daughter had opened a few years ago.

Ilsa must've anticipated Holly's question because she said, "Mandy is back in town. She offered to let me take my vacation time through New Year's. And since I haven't had a vacation in five years, I jumped on it."

Holly's eyes widened at the mention of Mrs. Pottson's daughter being back in Christmas Grove. She'd run off to Europe with her long-distance girlfriend four years ago, and no one had seen her since. "Mandy is back? Did her girlfriend come with her?"

"I don't think so. She looks like hell," Ilsa said with a sigh. "It's pretty clear she wants to throw herself into work at the store, so I told her she could call me if she needed anything or wanted me to come in, but otherwise I am happy to get a break. But that's not why I came by."

Holly set two plates on the table and the pair of them sat opposite each other as Holly said, "You're just full of gossip today, aren't you? I can't wait to hear this."

Ilsa chuckled and took a bite of the omelet. Her eyes rolled into the back of her head as she let out a contented sigh. "I should come by for breakfast more often."

Holly had a vision of her, Rex, and Ilsa all at the breakfast table and shook her head. "Maybe put that off until January?"

Ilsa threw her head back and cackled. "Got it. But maybe after the ball I'll have my own breakfast plans anyway."

"Oh? Did something happen with Zach?" Holly asked with both eyebrows raised. "Or did some new hottie walk into your life while I was busy dealing with—"

"Dealing with Rex? Please, girl. You weren't dealing with anything. You were getting your freak on."

Holly rolled her eyes but couldn't help the bubble of laughter that escaped her lips. "I was going to say dealing with the toy drive collections, but you might have a point about Rex taking up my time, too. Enough of that. It's time for you to spill your guts. Who are you anticipating spending your mornings with?"

"Zach," she said with a dreamy sigh. "I ran into him last night, and he asked me to the ball. If I can keep myself from acting like a bumbling idiot, maybe we can finally get this thing that's been bubbling between us to go somewhere."

Holly reached over and patted her friend's hand. "You just need to relax a little. Once you do that, I'm sure everything will go great."

"I hope so." She dug into the omelet again. "Because if I have to watch you cozying up to Rex for the foreseeable future while I sit home alone watching every sappy Christmas movie ever made, I might gain forty pounds from the sheer vats of chocolate required to keep me from drowning myself in cocktails."

"There's nothing wrong with sappy Christmas movies," Holly pointed out. "In fact, I've been saving them in my DVR for when I have the chance for a binge marathon. What are you doing Saturday? I have the day off. We could bake and snuggle on the couch all day?"

"It's a date." Ilsa took a sip of her coffee. "But we need to shop for dresses for the Christmas ball, too."

"Shopping first, movies and cookies after," Holly said with a firm nod, because no one wanted to try on a dress after they gorged themselves on fresh baked cookies.

CHAPTER 15

*R*ex parked his truck across the street from Charming Cookie's and hopped out into the cold night. Once the sun disappeared behind the foothills, the temperature dropped quickly in Christmas Grove. He shoved his hands into his jacket pockets, hunched his shoulders against the wind, and strode across the street, more than ready to lay eyes on the woman who'd stolen his heart. He'd spent the last four nights in her bed, and each morning it had been harder and harder to drag himself to work.

He'd been surprised to realize that his desire to spend time with her wasn't even driven by the physical aspect either. Rex just craved Holly's company. There was something about her smile, her laugh, her ability to center him that had him wanting to spend as much time with her as possible. Hanging out with her in her Victorian made him feel more at home than anywhere else, even Amelia's. It was strange, in a way, since he'd been such a wanderer for so long. Ever since his breakup with Sara, he'd been unable to stay in one place for any length of time. It seemed that as soon as he settled in, he was ready to move on to the next town, the next job. And considering he'd been in Christmas Grove for a few weeks already, he'd expected to be feeling the tug for some place new.

So far, it hadn't come. He supposed it would eventually. It always did. But this feeling he had while with Holly in her beautiful Victorian... It was different. Welcome even. And something he hoped wouldn't fade too quickly. It was why he wanted to savor his time with Holly. He wanted something to hold onto when it was time for him to make his move.

Rex walked through the door of Charming Cookie's and glanced around the deserted bakery. Prepackaged boxed cookies lined the shelves, and there was a colorful display of freshly baked items behind a glass case, but there wasn't a soul to be found in the lobby or behind the counter. He walked up to the checkout station and tapped a bell.

It took a few moments, but finally a small woman with tight gray curls hurried through the back-room door, shedding a pair of plastic gloves that looked to be covered in dough. "Well, hello there, handsome," she said, peering up at him with moony eyes. She was looking at him with such adoration that he swore he could almost see heart emojis pulsing where her pupils should be.

Rex held back a chuckle. It wasn't everyday someone so blatantly admired him. So what if she looked to be in her eighties? He'd take the ego boost. "Hey there. Is Holly Reineer teaching a baking class tonight?"

"She sure is." The older woman leaned on the counter and covered his hand with hers. "Did you reserve a spot?"

"Ah, no. Holly said I could just drop in." He pulled his hand away and slid it back into his jacket pocket.

The woman pouted a little but recovered quickly and

gestured for him to come around the counter. She opened the door and waved him in. "The classes are held back here."

Rex waited for her to go first and followed her into a hallway. The bakery kitchen was on the right, and to the left there was a door that led to a bright white classroom.

"Come on, dear," the lady said, taking his hand in hers and tugging him into the room.

Rex glanced around and smiled when he noted that all of the stations were filled with a student. Looked like he was going to be hanging with Holly after all. His eyes met hers, and he smiled as she blushed furiously. *Damn, that was cute as hell.*

"Rex! Hi," someone with a high-pitched voice called from his right.

The voice was familiar, but Rex didn't place it right away. He turned and first spotted Lily with her arm around her son Evan. The kid was grinning up at him.

"Are you going to learn to bake, too?" Evan asked.

"Sure am, little man," Rex said, crouching down next to him. "Is this your first lesson?"

Evan nodded.

"Mine, too. How is it so far? Is Holly a decent teacher?" He glanced up at his girl and winked. She rolled her eyes as she strode over to them.

"She's the best!" Evan declared and ran to hug Holly.

Rex grinned at both of them, his heart nearly melting at seeing the kid so animated after he'd been so emotional the other day when he gave up his stuffed wolf. "That's good to hear."

"Evan," Lily said, gently pulling her son from Holly's embrace. "We're interrupting the class. Let's go back to your station and—" Her phone rang, and she frowned as she looked at the screen. "Oh, no. It's my boss. I have to take this." She turned to Evan. "We need to step outside and let them get on with the class."

"But, Mom, I can't leave. My cookies aren't done yet," he protested.

"Honey, we have to take this call." She answered the phone and asked her boss to give her a moment. Leaning down to her son, she lowered her voice and said, "Come on, Evan, I can't leave you here without supervision."

Rex stared down at the disappointment on the kid's face and said, "I can watch him. I don't have a station anyway. Will it work for you if I give you a hand, buddy?"

"Yes!" Evan turned his big wide eyes on his mother. "Rex can watch me, right Mom?"

Lily gave Rex a grateful smile and nodded at her son. "Just be a good boy, Evan. Listen to Rex. I'll be back in a few minutes." She put the phone against her ear and hurried out of the classroom.

Rex slid behind the workstation with Evan and turned his attention to Holly. She beamed at him, and then her expression turned tender as she glanced at Evan. When she looked back at him, she mouthed, *Thank you* and then clasped her hands together.

"Okay, class. Sorry about the interruption. Let's get back to it."

Time flew by as Rex helped Evan mix his cookie batter, roll it out with a fancy rolling pin that left intricate designs in the dough, and then cut it into snowflakes with the cookie cutters Holly had provided. He hadn't even noticed that Lily had been gone for more than twenty minutes until she ran back into the room flustered and apologizing for disappearing for so long.

"My boss is having a crisis, and it looks like I'm going to need to go in and help him," Lilly said, giving her son a pained glance. "I'm sorry, Evan, but we need to go. I'll have to drop you off at Millie's house."

The boy frowned as his eyes darted over the raw cookies he'd so carefully rolled and cut. "But my cookies aren't done."

"Rex will finish them for you, sweetie. I'm really sorry. I know you were looking forward to this class, but I really have no choice. The computer is on the fritz again, and Mr. Fredrick is having trouble completing payroll."

There was a slight panic in her tone, which made Rex think that she was worried they wouldn't get paid. And with Christmas around the corner, it was enough to stress out any parent. Rex reached out and touched her shoulder. "I don't mean to butt in where I'm not wanted, but if you don't mind, I can take Evan to Millie's house after the class is over."

"Oh, no. I couldn't ask you to do that," Lily insisted, grabbing Evan's jacket from the back of his chair.

"You're not asking. I'm volunteering," Rex said, trying to appear as harmless as possible. "I know we don't know each other well, but Holly and Zach can vouch for me. Really, it's no trouble at all. We're having fun here."

With the class busy cutting out their cookies with cookie cutters, Holly strode over to them. "Is everything all right, Lily?"

There was concern in her lovely green gaze, and Rex felt a tenderness for her that made him want to pull her into his arms. He refrained though, not wanting to put on a display in front of her class.

"I have to head into work to make sure payroll happens, which means I need to pull Evan out of class." Lily bit down on her bottom lip as she eyed Rex, clearly torn on what she should do.

"I offered to be his baking buddy and drop him off at the

sitter on the way home," Rex said, shoving his hands into his pockets and rocking back on his heels.

Holly gave him a soft smile and patted his arm. "That's awfully sweet of you." She turned to Lily. "That sounds like a plan. I was going to ask Rex for a ride home tonight, so I'll be with them."

She was? Rex briefly wondered what happened to her car, but then decided her misfortune was his gain. Maybe he'd take her out for a late dinner after they dropped Evan off.

Lily let out a sigh of relief. "Really? That would be great." She gave her son a hug, told him to behave for Rex and Holly, and then gave Holly one last grateful smile as she rushed out of the class.

Rex placed his hand on the kid's shoulder. "Looks like it's back to work for us, kid."

Evan raised his fist in the air and pulled it down while whispering under his breath, "Yes!"

"These look fantastic, Evan," Holly said, inspecting the raw cookies that were already on a tray waiting to go into the oven. "You've been practicing."

He nodded. "Millie lets me come over and bake with her sometimes."

"I bet she appreciates your help very much." Holly ruffled his hair. "I'm glad your night wasn't cut short. These snowflake cookies are likely to be the star of the evening."

Evan beamed up at her, and it wasn't hard to see that the kid looked at her with some sort of hero worship. Rex couldn't blame him. Holly had it all and more.

"I've got to keep making my rounds," Holly continued. "I can't wait to see what these look like once they're done." She brushed her hand down one of Rex's arms, and then moved on to see what the rest of the class was up to.

Rex spent the next hour and a half helping Evan create the most gorgeous snowflake sugar cookies. But he had to admit, the kid didn't need him. He already knew what he was doing. It wasn't long before the cookies were done baking and had been dusted with powdered sugar, giving them a frosted look. Rex helped Evan pack his cookies away in a plastic container, all of them except one.

"Holly looks like she's finishing up. Are you ready?" Rex asked Evan.

He nodded, holding the cookie carefully in a napkin.

"Okay. Let's go get her." Rex carried the container of cookies and followed Evan as he made his way to her at the front of the room.

"I'm almost ready," she said, smiling at them.

"Okay." Evan stood right in front of her, holding his cookie.

After she had her jacket on and her purse in hand, she turned to them. "How was the class? Did you enjoy it?"

Evan nodded his head and held the cookie out to her.

"Is this for me?" she asked, her eyes sparkling with pride.

"Yes." The kid grinned up at her, and Rex felt something stir in his chest. There was just something about her interaction with the boy that touched him.

"It's amazing, Evan," she said almost reverently as she studied it. "Really gorgeous. Did Rex help you make this?"

Evan looked back at Rex and blinked before he turned back to Holly. "No."

"He did it all himself. I was just there as a helper," Rex said. "The dude has skills."

"Yes. He does." Holly crouched down, stared him in the eye, and said, "Evan, I do believe you're my star student. This might be the best cookie I've seen in this class. Heck, all year. I'm impressed."

Evan beamed at her. And as the three of them walked out of the classroom, Rex felt... fulfilled, as if he was right where he was supposed to be for the first time in his life. He placed a hand on the small of Holly's back and let the moment just soak in. Never had anything felt more perfect. And he wanted it to last for forever.

CHAPTER 16

*H*olly glanced over her shoulder at Evan sitting in the back seat of Rex's truck. The kid had a brilliant smile on his face as he stared out the window at the holiday decorations in the neighborhood. Instead of taking him straight to Millie's house, Rex had offered to take them around to see what new Christmas lights had gone up over the last week or so. And the town proved to be nothing short of spectacular. It seemed everyone, even grumpy old Fred Jenkins, had a lit-up wire reindeer set in their yard this year. Holly couldn't recall Fred ever getting into the festivities of the season before.

"Did you help your mom decorate your house, Evan?" Holly asked him.

The boy nodded. "We don't have anything fancy, but me and mom put lights in all of the bushes, and we made a wreath for the door."

"I bet it's beautiful," she said, just imagining what he'd come up with. Evan was her star pupil in her Wednesday night baking class. And what was even more remarkable was the fact that she knew Lily had extremely limited baking supplies. No cookie cutters, no rolling pin, and definitely no electric mixer. Fancy tools that make it easier for Evan to make intricate snowflakes were completely out of the budget for Lily. And still, Evan managed to be so creative with basic cutlery and poster board cutouts that his creations were always the most unique and beautiful.

The boy truly had the talent of an artist. It was why she let him join her class for free every week. There was no way there was extra in Lily's budget for the class, and it warmed Holly's heart to be able to pay a bit of kindness forward. Besides, she loved having him in class. His creations always put a smile on her face.

"It's okay," Evan said, still pressing his face to the window.

Holly glanced over at Rex. His face was hidden in the shadows of the evening, but she could still make out the sharp line of his jaw. She wanted to slide over and press herself to his side. He'd been wonderful that evening with Evan. The fact that he'd so seamlessly stepped in to help Lily and Evan had turned her heart to pure mush. "You're a good sport," she whispered to him. "You know that, right?"

He chuckled softly and reached over to gently squeeze her thigh. "I enjoyed myself, Hols. In fact, I can't wait for the next baking lesson. How about tomorrow night?"

"The next class isn't until next Wednesday," Evan chirped from the back.

"He's right," Holly said with a solemn nod. "If you want a private lesson, it's going to cost extra."

"Extra, huh?" Rex said, his voice huskier than normal as he let his gaze slide over her.

A tingle traveled up Holly's spine, and she glanced away

from him just to settle herself. Now was not the time to be lusting after him. Not with Evan still in the car

"I'm sure we can work something out," Rex said, still flirting with her.

She just nodded and took Evan's lead by staring at Christmas Grove's abundance of Christmas lights and decorations. By the time Rex pulled into Millie's driveway, Evan had dozed off. Holly started to reach back to wake the kid, but Rex stopped her.

"No. Let him sleep. I'll carry him into Millie's." He jumped out of the truck, jogged around to the passenger side, and tugged a limp Evan out of the truck. The boy snuggled into Rex's arms as the pair made their way up to Millie's front door.

Holly would've gone with Rex, but just as she'd been about to open her own door, a familiar hazy feeling clouded her brain, making her head spin a little. She sucked in a deep breath and waited for the inevitable vision to come. Her vision turned fuzzy just as it always did, and then she was plunged into a world of vibrant sound and colors. Her visions were always so clear and focused, there was never a chance for misinterpretation. To her, that was both a blessing and a curse.

"Good afternoon, little dude," Rex said as he leaned over a crib. The sweet sounds of a baby cooing filled her ears, making what was left of Holly's heart nearly shatter from the heartbreaking sweetness of it all. "Ready for our play time before Mommy gets home?"

Rex lifted the child out of the crib and settled his sweet little face against his shoulder while gently cupping the baby's head. The move was so tender and sweet that it was impossible to keep the tears from pooling in her eyes.

Then it hit her. She didn't recognize the house, and when she glanced out the window, the town definitely wasn't Christmas Grove. The small cottage was in the middle of a village of other cute small cottages with redwoods in the distance.

The baby let out a tiny wail, and Rex shushed him. "It's okay. I've got you, little one."

Holly snapped back to reality and pressed a hand to her stomach as the nausea took over.

Rex was going to be a daddy, and Holly clearly wasn't in the picture. Physical pain shot through her chest, and suddenly it was hard to breathe. She rolled the window down and gasped in air.

Calm down, she ordered herself. This was always going to be a short-term relationship. Of course Rex was going to move on with his life. And didn't she want that for him? He deserved a family if he wanted one. Only the Rex she'd gotten to know over the last week didn't seem like a man who was looking to settle down.

She turned her attention to Millie's house, recalling Rex holding Evan close as he carried him inside. The man had everything he needed to be a good father. After watching him with Evan that night, it was more than obvious. He just needed to meet the right woman.

A small sob got caught in the back of Holly's throat, but she forced herself to swallow through it. Even though Rex hadn't looked as if he'd aged at all in her vision, that didn't mean anything. The scene could've been five years down the road. He was only in his thirties. It wasn't as if he was going to age overnight.

The front door opened, and Rex hurried out back to the truck. He jumped in and grinned at her. "Evan is already crashed out in Millie's guest room. But he did manage to wake up long enough to tell me to thank you for him."

A WITCH FOR MR. HOLIDAY

Holly let out a small startled laugh. "Of course he did. Lily has certainly done her job on teaching him manners. He's a true joy."

Rex reached over and grabbed her hand, tugging gently. "Come over here."

She didn't hesitate. After her vision, she needed to feel him against her, remind herself that what they had right now was real and, no matter what else happened in the future, she didn't need to cheat herself out of enjoying his company for as long as it lasted.

Rex's arm landed on her shoulders and he pulled her in tightly to his side, pressing a kiss to her head. "Have you eaten?"

She shook her head as she focused on the hundreds of tiny white lights glowing from the trees and bushes in both Millie's and Lily's yards. Evan had been spot-on. The decorations weren't elaborate in any way, but they were festive and that was enough. "No. Not since a power bar at lunch."

"Are you up for dinner out, or do you want me to whip something up back at your place?" He put the truck in gear and backed it out of Millie's driveway.

"I could go out," she said, needing something to distract her from the crushing vision she'd just had. "How about Noelle's? They have an incredible seafood risotto."

"Noelle's it is," he said, running his hand down her arm before returning it to the steering wheel and navigating back to Main Street.

The small farm-to-table restaurant was housed in an old oversized cottage that had worn wooden floors and a gorgeous exposed-beam ceiling. Since it was a Wednesday night, it wasn't too difficult to get a table and before long, they were seated next to a floor-to-ceiling window that looked out over the 650-acre lake. Twinkling lights lit the large pier as well as most of the boats moored at the marina. There was even a red carpet lining the pier, as well as wreaths on each of the pilings. It looked as if they were ready to welcome Santa himself.

Holly couldn't help but smile as she gazed down at the moonlight-kissed lake. The water rippled peacefully, and she finally thought she might understand why Mrs. Pottson's polar bear club was so enamored with jumping naked into the bitter cold water all winter. It looked... cleansing, as if the purity would just strip all your troubles away. Maybe she should join them on their next dip.

"What's wrong, Holly?" Rex asked, pulling her out of her thoughts.

"Huh? Nothing. Just hungry," she lied.

Rex pushed the plate of goat cheese turnovers toward her. She'd ordered them as an appetizer and promptly forgot all about them while brooding over her vision.

"Thanks." She forced a smile and slid one of the turnovers onto her plate. "How did you like the baking class?"

"Loved it." Rex plucked a piece of sourdough from the breadbasket. "Can't say I did anything other than assist Evan, but that's cool. That kid has some chops."

Holly nodded. "He really does. I love that kid."

"What do you say to outfitting him with fancy baking tools for his secret Santa gift? He told me he has to go to Millie's to practice and even then, she only has the basics."

Damn. Why did that man have to make her heart melt multiple times a day? Holly leaned forward, staring him in the eye, and gave him a watery smile. "I think that is the best idea ever. He is going to love that."

Rex moved in, meeting her halfway, and pressed his lips to hers. "You're amazing. You know that?"

She laughed. "Why? Because I can bake cookies?"

"No." He squeezed her hand lightly. "I mean, yes. You're excellent at that, but I was talking about your heart. The way you're so kind to Lily and Evan. The fact you let him take your classes and how encouraging you are. It's beautiful, Hols. I love your generosity. Love how warm you are to those around you. And most of all, I'm grateful you've let me into your life for this season." He lifted her hand and placed a kiss on her palm. "Thank you."

His words lit her up inside, pushing out all of the earlier anxiety... right up until he said he was grateful to be in her life *for this season*. He had no way of knowing that she felt gut-punched, as if he'd pushed the one button that was making her queasy. But still, she lifted her gaze, looked him right in the eye, forced herself to give him an easy smile, and said, "You're very welcome, Rex. Now I have a question for you."

"What's that?" he asked, his eyes riveted to hers.

"Are you going to eat that other goat cheese turnover, or am I going to have to throw myself on it? Because it would be a crime to let it go to waste."

Rex's eyes sparkled as he laughed and pushed the turnover closer to her. "You better eat it. I don't think my manly waistline can handle it."

She shrugged, picked up the turnover, and said, "Your loss."

CHAPTER 17

"Breakfast!" Rex called as he slid a small stack of pancakes onto a plate. After pouring Holly a cup of coffee, he placed the plate and mug on the table then retreated to grab his own plate and a second cup of coffee for himself. After doctoring his java with some cream, he sat down across from Holly and gazed at her as he took a sip.

"It's too early to be staring. I bet I still have sleep in my eyes," Holly said, pouring real maple syrup over her pancakes.

His body shook with silent laughter. "After the way you woke me up this morning? Not likely."

Holly's sweet face turned a lovely shade of red, and she tilted her head so that a sheet of her hair would hide her eyes.

Rex just grinned at her. He'd awoken with her hands on him, and after a couple of soft kisses, they'd lost themselves in one another. It was by far his favorite way to wake up in the morning. It was also a relief, because it hadn't escaped his notice that Holly had been a little out of sorts ever since the night they'd taken Evan home. She hadn't been upset with him, that had been apparent, but she'd been slightly distant. This morning was a different matter altogether. She was relaxed, and her eyes were bright and sparkling as if she just couldn't wait to get on with her day. It was magnetizing, and she was pulling him in just by staring at him over her coffee mug. "What's got you in such a good mood this morning, Hols?"

Her blush deepened, but she just smiled at him and forked a bite of pancakes into her mouth.

"I see. Well, I wouldn't mind waking up like that every day."

"I bet," she said with a small, secretive smile.

While Rex was relieved and more than happy that she'd shaken off whatever was bothering her, he was still curious and wondered if he should ask her about it again. He'd tried the night before, but she'd brushed him off, indicating it had just been a long week. And maybe she'd been telling the truth. Since they'd slept in and had a leisurely morning in bed, she seemed one hundred percent herself again. "What do you have planned for today?"

"Shopping with Ilsa. Want to meet me afterward so we can get Evan's secret Santa gift? There's a fancy kitchen shop on Main Street that should have everything we need."

"Sure. I've got a few things to do for Zach's tree farm, then I'm free. Text me when you're ready for me to head down there?" he asked.

"Will do."

Rex savored their time at breakfast, and when she was ready to go, he walked her to her front door. "I'll get the dishes done and check on Sabrina before I go."

Her expression softened, and she pressed her palm to his cheek. After kissing him lightly on the lips, she said, "You don't have to do that. Leave the dishes. I'll get to them when I get home. And I already fed and watered Sabrina."

"I don't mind." Rex slipped his arms around the beautiful

woman who'd so seamlessly let him into her life. "And when I'm done, I'll let Sabrina run around a little. Go. Have a good time with Ilsa. You deserve it."

"You're too good to me," she said, but the words sounded almost sad.

He frowned and brushed a lock of hair out of her eyes. "Holly. I wish you'd just tell me what's been bothering you."

She opened her mouth, closed it, and then shook her head as she squeezed her eyelids closed. "You're right. I should tell you. But not right now. There's no time. Tonight? After all the shopping's done, maybe we can take a walk if it isn't bitter cold."

"All right. That sounds like a plan." His voice was quiet now. He hated the idea of waiting all day to find out what was on her mind, but he didn't have a choice. He'd waited three days already. One more wasn't going to kill him. Rex leaned in and kissed her forehead. "I'd love a walk with you. Go on now. You don't want to keep Ilsa waiting."

She let out a tiny huff of laughter. "Ten bucks says that even if I'm late I'll still be waiting on her."

"I'm not fool enough to take that bet," he said, giving her a half smile and walking her backward out onto the porch. "Now get going. I have a date with your bunny."

Her smile turned into a grin. "Give her kisses for me, will you?"

She was so damned cute standing there in her wool coat and handwoven scarf. If she'd had a mug in her hand, she'd have looked like an advertisement for hot cocoa or something. He couldn't help but muss her up a little. Without giving her a moment to react, he pulled her back into his arms, buried his hands in her thick red hair, and kissed her so thoroughly that when he finally broke away from her they were both breathing hard. He pressed his thumb to her bottom lip, grinned at her, and said, "You're definitely going to be late now."

"It was worth it." She pressed up on her toes and kissed him one last time before tearing herself away and trotting down the stairs to her car. Without looking back, she jumped in and sped down the driveway.

"So. This is what your mornings look like now," said a familiar male voice from the side of the house.

Rex glanced over to find Zach leaning against the house, his arms crossed over his chest and one ankle hooked over the other. "Have you taken up being a creeper as a hobby now, Zach?"

His friend laughed and pushed himself off the wall. "No, but it's tempting after that public display of affection."

"We had no idea we had an audience." Rex held the door open for Zach. "Need a cup of coffee?"

"Sure." The man pulled a knitted cap off his head, making his dark hair stand up at crazy angles. He ran a hand over his skull, trying to tame them, but it was a useless gesture. He looked like he'd just rolled out of bed, stuffed a hat on his head, and made his way to Holly's.

Once they were back in the kitchen, Rex poured a couple more cups of coffee, handed one to his friend, and moved to the sink to clean up the breakfast dishes. "So, wanna tell me why you trekked your way over here instead of just calling me?"

"I did try to call you," Zach said and took a sip of the coffee. "Damn this is good. Did Holly make it?"

Rex smirked. "No, I did."

Zach raised one eyebrow. "You make coffee this good, and you haven't been sharing with me every morning? I should make that a new requirement of your employment."

Rolling his eyes, Rex said, "If you want me to bring you coffee, all you need to do is ask, jackass. Supply me with a travel mug, and I'll make it happen."

"Done." Zach took another long sip of his coffee and then turned to his friend. "Amelia called the office phone looking for you."

Rex dropped the pan he'd been scrubbing back into the sink and turned to Zach, worry clawing in his gut. His sister was not one for phone calls. Texting was her thing. Rex was fairly certain she'd rather cease communications altogether rather than be forced to actually call someone. "What did she say? Is something wrong?" He heard the panic in his tone, but couldn't seem to shake it as he continued, "Is she in trouble?"

"She didn't say she was. I was still in the house. She left a message that you're to call her back." He frowned. "It didn't sound like she was in trouble, but it did sound as if it might be important. Like she just needed to talk to you."

"Dammit." Rex patted his pockets for his phone and came up empty. He knew he'd had it last night, which meant it had to be upstairs. And if Amelia was already looking for him through Zach's landline, the call had to be important. Without a word, he turned and jogged through the house and up the stairs to Holly's bedroom. He took a few moments to scan the floor, searching for the phone he knew had to be there. When he didn't find it right away, he dropped down on all fours and peered under the bed.

"There." He reached out and grabbed the phone only to find that the battery had died. "Oh, hell." After stuffing the phone into his pocket, he jogged back downstairs and found Zach at the sink, finishing the dishes. "What are you doing, man?"

Zach shrugged. "Helping out."

"I can do that." Rex didn't know why, but he really didn't

like watching his friend washing dishes at Holly's sink. It probably had something to do with the familiarity or the fact of seeing another man engaging in something domestic in her domain. He felt territorial.

"Nah." Zach waved a hand. "Call your sister. I'm almost done here."

"Can't. My phone is dead. Need to head back to the office so I can charge this thing."

Zach nodded, placed the last plate in the dishwasher, and then turned off the water. "Then let's go."

Rex glanced at Sabrina the rabbit, noted she was curled up sleeping, and silently vowed to get her out of her cage that night to let her stretch her legs. After grabbing his jacket off the back of one of the chairs, Rex strode to the back door and waved for Zach to follow him. "It's shorter if we go out this way."

Zach laughed. "You think I don't know that? Either Holly or her grandmother have been my neighbor my entire life."

"Right." Rex shoved his hands into his jacket pockets and bent his head against the December wind as he trudged along the path that led to Zach's office.

"Wanna talk about what's going on with Holly?" Zach asked.

Rex jerked his head in Zach's direction. "What are you talking about? What's going on?"

Zach frowned and drew his eyebrows together in obvious confusion. "I was thinking you might tell me. From here it looks like you two have gotten really friendly. I mean, you've been staying over at her house every night for almost a week now, right?"

"Are you keeping tabs on me?" Rex asked, side-eyeing his friend.

Zach rolled his eyes. "Hardly, but I can't miss your walk of shame every morning when you literally walk right by my office window."

"Oh." Rex laughed. "I didn't realize you were going into work that early."

He shrugged one shoulder. "Usually, I don't. But when I have trouble sleeping, I go into the office and catch up on administration stuff. It's been a little rough lately. But on the upside, the bookkeeping has never looked better."

Rex glanced over at his friend. "What's keeping you up at night? Or should I say who?"

"I don't want to talk about it." Zach stared straight ahead. "How are my trees coming? Any progress?"

Rex almost ignored the question and asked if Zach's issue had to do with Ilsa. But then he just let it go. If he'd told Zach he didn't want to talk about something, he'd resent the hell out of him if he kept pushing. "They're showing improvement. Won't know for another week or so if I have to modify my treatments, but so far so good."

Zach nodded and unlocked the office door, waving Rex in.

Warm air engulfed him as Rex strode into the slightly cluttered space. There was a laptop set up on a desk in the corner with an office phone to the right. Invoices had been neatly stacked into three piles, just waiting to be filed away. And while there were a couple of empty coffee mugs and a plate with crumbs on it, the rest of the space had been cleared as if Zach had been spending a lot of time in the office. It wasn't clean by any stretch of the imagination, but it was organized for the first time since Rex had arrived.

Zach grabbed the plate and the mugs. "I'm headed into the house. Need anything? I've got fresh muffins from the Enchanted Bean Stalk. Cream cheese cranberry."

"Sure," Rex said, plugging in his phone to charge. As Zach exited the office, Rex picked up the landline, scrolled through the caller IDs listed on the phone, and pressed his sister's number. It went straight to voicemail. "Dammit." After the recording, he left a message indicating that his phone had been dead and to call him back as soon as she had a chance. He glanced at his phone, which had already come back online, and texted her the same message.

He had just sat at Zach's desk, getting ready to go over his notes for the trees that needed his attention, when there was a knock on the door. Rex got up, assuming Zach's hands were too full to work the knob, and pulled the door open. "That was fast—" He stopped talking when he saw that the man at the door wasn't Zach. He was a tall, dark-haired man with piercing blue eyes and a two-day beard. He looked like someone who should be in a cologne ad or something, not someone who would be roaming around Zach's Christmas tree farm during the off hours. The place didn't open until noon and stayed open until nine o'clock to accommodate the working families that came to the farm to pick out a tree. "Sorry. I was expecting someone else. Can I help you?"

The stranger gave Rex a disarming smile and said, "Sorry. I know you're not open yet, but I was hoping someone would be here. I need a really tall Christmas tree, and it's a surprise for my fiancée. Do you think you could help me out? I'm kind of in the doghouse, and this gesture would go a long way to win her over, I think."

"Sure," Rex said, giving the stranger an easy smile. "What'd ya do? Forget an important anniversary or something?" The comment was light and delivered with a chuckle, but when the man frowned and nodded while pressing two fingers to his forehead, Rex backpedaled. "Oh, sorry. I didn't mean to get personal. Let's just get you that tree."

The man blew out a breath. "Don't worry about it. It's my own fault. Let's just hope this does the trick, huh? My girl is a sucker for everything Christmas. She's always talked about wanting a second, larger tree for her front yard, so I figured this was the best way to get her attention."

Rex knew a little something about women who were crazy for Christmas. Or at least one. Holly had said something about wanting a tree in every room of her house. When he'd offered to help her with that, she'd waved him off, saying she didn't have enough decorations and that the Great Hall was plenty this year. Since she'd seemed to mean it, he'd let it go. But now he was wondering if he should do what this guy was doing and just surprise her. Only he wasn't in the doghouse. Or at least he wasn't as far as he knew. He still wondered what had been bothering Holly, but considering the affection she'd had for him, he didn't think it had to do with him.

"Sounds like it can't hurt," Rex said. "Let's go find you a tree."

CHAPTER 18

"*What* do you think of this one?" Ilsa asked, twirling in front of the dressing room mirror. The form-fitting, sleeveless, ankle-length dress shimmered under the fluorescent lights. It was red and showed off her flawless pale skin, making her look like a supermodel.

"It's gorgeous," Holly said.

Ilsa sighed. "That's what you said about the last three."

"That's because you look gorgeous in all of them." Holly walked over to the rack where Ilsa had hung her collection of possibilities. They were all different colors and different lengths. A couple were sleeveless, one had spaghetti straps, and the last one had sweet cap sleeves. But the one thing they had in common was that each and every one of them shimmered with sparkles. "You're going to be the center of attention no matter what you wear."

"I only care about what Zach thinks," Ilsa insisted. "I feel like this is my last chance to not make a fool of myself."

Holly raised one eyebrow at her friend. "What's the goal

again? To get him to date you or take you home at the end of the night?"

Ilsa raised her chin and narrowed her eyes at Holly. "Why can't it be both? We're liberated women, aren't we?"

Holly couldn't help it. She laughed. "Of course we are. Sorry. I didn't mean it like that. I was just wondering how you hoped the night would end, because that changes my advice."

"Well, I'm open to possibilities, but I'm certainly not going to complain if we end up having a sleep over," she said with a mischievous glint in her eyes.

"The red one then. It's doing some fabulous things for your boobs." Holly lifted her friend's long mane of hair and twisted it up to sit on top of her head. "Hair up. Make sure he can see your long neck and miles of skin. I think that should do the trick."

"You know something, Hols?" Ilsa asked as she met her friend's eyes in the mirror.

"What's that?" Holly let Ilsa's hair fall down her back and picked up a pair of silver high heels for Ilsa to try on.

"You're a good friend. And not nearly as goody-two-shoes as some people in this town might believe." Ilsa tugged the red dress up and slipped her feet into the silver shoes. "Perfect. I think you could be a stylist."

"Only for you. It's easy when your subject could be a literal supermodel." She retreated and plucked the sparkling silver, old-Hollywood-style dress off a rack. "Do you think I can do this justice?"

"Yes. Get your butt in the dressing room and try it on already."

Holly stared at it and smiled to herself. It had a square neckline, was fitted at the waist, and had a full skirt. It was gorgeous, like something she could see Audrey Hepburn wearing to the Oscars.

"Add a waist-length white jacket, and you'll be the starlet of the ball," Ilsa said.

Holly sighed. "It would be wonderful wouldn't it?"

"I happen to have one in stock," Kasey, the store owner, said from behind them. "Want me to grab it?"

"Yes," Ilsa said without hesitation.

Kasey grinned and took off back into her store.

"How am I going to afford all of this?" Holly asked.

"Just splurge, Hols. You never spend money on yourself. Don't you think it's about time for you to do something nice for yourself for once?" Ilsa stepped into her dressing room and a second later, Holly heard the zipper of her dress.

"A splurge is one thing. Going broke is entirely another." Holly took her dress into her own dressing room and nearly gasped out loud once she had the dress on. It fit perfectly and did amazing things for her figure.

The curtain on her dressing room flew open, and Ilsa stood there in her jeans and sweater. "I heard that gasp."

Holly watched Ilsa's eyes widen in the mirror, and a slow smile claimed her lips. She was right. The dress was made for her.

"You are buying that even if you have to put it on three credit cards." Ilsa moved in closer and then threw her arms around Holly. "He's going to have a stroke when he sees you in that. I don't think I've ever seen anything more beautiful."

"Oh, wow," another voice said from behind them.

Holly turned and spotted Kasey holding a silver faux fur jacket as well as a white wool one.

"I brought choices," Kasey said.

"The faux fur one," Ilsa said decisively and tugged it out of

Kasey's hands. "Here." She held it up for Holly to slip her arms into it.

The silky fur was soft on Holly's skin and made her feel like a million bucks. But when she saw the full effect in the dressing room mirror, Holly's eyes stung with tears. The look was so elegant she could've been royalty.

"We'll take it," Ilsa said.

Holly glanced down at the price tag and let out a gasp. "Ilsa. I can't. It's too—"

"Consider it your Christmas present. You have to have this, sweetie. Don't fight me on this. I'll just come back and buy it for you anyway."

"Ilsa," she whispered as her eyes filled with tears. "You're too good to me."

"Probably." Ilsa laughed. "But I love you, and you love me, so it is what it is." She turned to Kasey. "Great find. It's perfect."

"No, you two are perfect," she said and let out a tiny sob. "Friendship goals."

After Kasey returned to the front of the shop, Holly and Ilsa looked at each other and neither could control the giggling.

"We're friendship goals, Hols," Ilsa said, wiping at her eyes. "It makes us sound eighty, don't you think?"

"Maybe a little." She gave her friend a crooked smile. "But I tell you what. You had better still be my bestie when we're racing golf carts across the old folk's home, giving the caregivers heart palpitations."

Ilsa giggled harder and held out her pinky to Holly. As Holly looped hers around Ilsa's they both said, "It's a pact."

"Good." Holly gently pushed her friend out of her dressing room. "Now get out so I can get changed."

After they checked out, Ilsa nodded to Noelle's. "Let's get lunch."

"Sure." Holly followed her into the restaurant, smiling to herself as she remembered the last time she'd eaten there.

"You have that look on your face again," Ilsa said as soon as they sat down at a table next to a window.

"What look?" Holly nodded a thanks to the waiter who had immediately filled their water glasses.

Ilsa stared her in the eye and raised one eyebrow in some sort of challenge. "The one that says you're stupidly in love and ready to sacrifice everything for a man you've only known for a few weeks."

Holly sighed. "This again? You've already made it quite clear that you think I'm going to get hurt. And we both decided I should enjoy myself. So that's what I'm doing. End of story."

"Holly." Ilsa closed her eyes and shook her head.

"Ilsa." Holly mimicked her friend's exasperated tone. "I'm not the only one putting my heart on the line. What about you and Zach?"

"I'm not on the verge of following Zach across the country." She sat back in her chair and crossed her arms over her chest, waiting for Holly to take the bait.

Holly rolled her eyes. "I'm not going anywhere and we both know it. Stop borrowing trouble."

"Is that what I'm doing? Are you sure?"

A waitress came by to drop off a breadbasket and take their orders. Once she was gone, Holly leaned forward and said, "I know you're worried about this thing between me and Rex. But honestly, Ilsa, it's the most natural relationship I've ever had. It just feels right. More right than anything else. So walking away from him while he's here in Christmas Grove isn't an option."

"That's what worries me," she said, covering Holly's hand with one of her own. "I can see how much he means to you, babe. I just don't want you left in a million pieces when he leaves."

Holly let out a choked laugh. "I think that's a real possibility. But I'm in this anyway."

"Oh, hun." Ilsa squeezed her hand. "I see. Well, when you know his departure date, let me know. I'll be over with Ben and Jerry's, pizza, and a marathon of movies to last us through Valentine's day. Okay?"

One single tear ran down Holly's cheek as she nodded at her best friend. She knew she was going to be a major mess when Rex left. There was no denying it now. But Ilsa would help glue her back together. It's what besties did. "I love you."

"I love you, too. Now carb up." She handed Holly a piece of sourdough bread. "We have a lot more shopping to do this afternoon. You'll need your strength.

Holly chuckled as she smeared salted butter on her bread. "If you insist."

CHAPTER 19

*R*ex stood outside of Ginger's Tableau nearly freezing his tush off. The sun was starting to set behind the foothills and as usual, the temperature had fallen fast. He'd even heard there was a slight chance of snow that evening. It wouldn't be enough to cause any issues in Christmas Grove, but it meant a chilly night.

"Hey!" Holly's face was radiant as she bounded up to him, all smiles and glittering eyes.

"Hey, yourself. You look like you had a good day today." He pulled her to him and kissed her softly on the lips before letting her go.

"I did. Sorry it's so late. We got a little carried away." She slipped her arm through his and tugged him into the shop.

"It's all right. I ended up helping Zach around the Christmas tree lot. There were a lot of families rushing to get their tree before it gets too close to Christmas." The work had also distracted him from waiting for his sister to call back. It had been hours of radio silence. He couldn't help the worry that had crept into his chest. But he'd refrained from calling their mother. He didn't want to worry her, too. If Amelia was in any real trouble, he was certain someone in the family would've already gotten in touch with him.

"That was nice of you." She pulled out a list she'd created. "These are the basic items we use in class. I was thinking we could get him all of these and an electric mixer. What do you think?"

"Sounds perfect." It didn't take long to fill up a shopping cart of basic baking tools. Some of them, Rex didn't even know what they were used for. But Holly did and that's all that mattered. Once they had everything on the list, they moved over to the mixing aisle. "How about a KitchenAid?" Rex said. "The one in my mother's kitchen has been there for twenty years."

Holly nodded. "Yeah. It's a solid choice."

As Rex put the box in their cart, he noticed Holly practically drooling over a Breville bread machine. He leaned over her shoulder and asked, "Have you taken up bread making?"

She chuckled. "Yes and no. I'd love to make more homemade bread, but I just don't have the time. I've been eyeing this one because it makes a great sourdough. Sadly, it's not in my budget."

Rex eyed the appliance and shrugged. "Well, if you're a good girl, maybe Santa will bring you one."

She turned and narrowed her eyes at him. "Do not even think about getting this for me. It's too much. Besides, I'm perfectly capable of making bread without it. This was just wishful thinking."

He held his hands up in a surrender motion. "Whoa. Don't look at me. I already got you something."

Her expression softened. "You did?"

"Sure." He jerked his head, indicating that she should follow him to the checkout counter. "Are you saying you haven't gotten me anything yet?"

Her face turned pink, and she swallowed before she stammered, "Um, I'm a last-minute shopper. Always have been."

He barked out a laugh. "I see. Well, if you need ideas, you know where to find me."

She rolled her eyes. "Just for that I'm going to get you a toiletry kit and fill it with deodorant, dental floss, and disposable hand wipes."

"That should be really useful actually." He winked at her and then turned his attention to the cashier.

When she rattled off the total, Holly grimaced. "Yikes. That's a small fortune. I never realized how much that stuff adds up."

"Good tools are worth every penny," Rex said, handing the cashier his credit card. "Do you think Evan will take care of this stuff?"

"Absolutely. You saw him in class. What do you think?"

Rex thought back to the way Evan carefully handled everything. His movements were deliberate, and he didn't do anything without intention. It was like watching an artist in his element. It was remarkable for any person, really, let alone a nine-year-old kid. "Yeah. He will. It seems as if he really appreciates everything he is given, too."

"He does." Holly nodded and laughed when she scanned the cart full of bags. "Lily is going to kill us. But she'll love us, too."

"Then it's worth it." Rex filled the back seat of his truck and then turned to her. "About that thing that's been bothering you. Can you share it now? I'm going a little crazy not knowing what's causing you such turmoil."

Holly glanced away, but when she turned back to him, she cupped his cheeks with both hands and said, "Isn't it obvious? I already know it's going to be hard to say goodbye when you leave. But then you go and do wonderful stuff like this..." Her voice trailed off. "It's hard knowing you're leaving. That's all."

Rex swallowed, barely able to make his throat work. "I don't want to cause you pain, Holly."

She shook her head. "You're not. But when it's time to say goodbye, it's going to suck."

He nodded. It was something he'd come to realize, too. Leaving Holly was going to make him feel like someone had ripped his heart right out of his chest. He wrapped his arms around Holly and held her tight. "I get it, Hols. I really do. I feel the same way."

She pulled back and looked up at him with a watery smile. "There's that at least. I'd hate to be the only miserable one."

Rex let out a breath and continued to caress her, not wanting to let go. Finally she was the one to break the connection.

"Follow me back to my house?" she asked.

Rex nodded, and once they pulled up to the front of her house, it took him a moment to notice something was off. Holly hadn't parked in her usual spot because there was already a truck there. A truck Rex recognized. The white Chevy crew cab had New York plates just like the one that belonged to the guy he'd helped that morning at Zach's tree farm. The same guy who'd said he wanted to surprise his fiancée with a large tree in her yard.

Rex's gaze slid over to a cleared section off to the right of the house, and sure enough, the giant tree had been erected and decorated with thousands of twinkling lights. It was impressive, and Rex's gut clenched as he spotted the tall man striding down off the porch toward Holly's car.

Without another thought, Rex jumped out of his truck just as Holly emerged from her car and slammed the door.

"Ryan? What the hell are you doing here?" Her voice was shaky, and her fists were clenched. There was no mistaking her anger.

"I told you I'd be back, Holly," the man said and flashed her a tender smile.

Rex wanted to wipe it right off his face. Why did he think Holly was his fiancée? Hadn't she told him something about her ex leaving and then never coming back? He'd broken things off in a card if he remembered correctly.

"Two years too late!" Holly shouted. Then she turned to Rex, her expression shell-shocked. "I..." She shook her head. "That's Ryan. I had no idea he was going to show up here like..." Waving a hand at the tree, she added, "Like this."

"Like how he showed up to sweep you off your feet in a grand gesture as if he hadn't abandoned you like you didn't matter at all?"

She let out a choked laugh. "Yeah. That."

"Hey. That's not what happened," Ryan scoffed as he stared at Rex. "Who the hell are you anyway? Wait." His brow wrinkled as he studied Rex. "Aren't you the guy from the Christmas tree farm?"

"Yep." He placed his hand on the small of Holly's back. "If I'd known you were trying to put the moves on my girl, I probably wouldn't have been as helpful."

Ryan scoffed. "Holly, you deserve better than a transient Christmas tree farm worker. Please tell me you're not really into this guy."

Rex let out a bark of laughter at the guy's complete

snobbery. He already knew Holly wasn't going to ignore that remark, so he just glanced down at her and raised one eyebrow while he waited.

"Don't be a jackass, Ryan," she said with a sigh. The wind picked up and she shivered from the cold.

Rex was about to suggest they go inside when his phone chimed with a text. Biting back a groan, he grabbed it from his pocket and read the message. It was from his sister. *I'm here in Christmas Grove at your cabin. Where are you?*

"What?" he gasped to himself.

"What's wrong?" Holly asked him.

"Nothing. Or at least not anything that I know of. My sister is here early." He tapped back a message, letting her know he was on his way, and then turned to Holly. "I have to go let her in my cabin. Are you okay here?" He glanced over at Ryan. "If you need me to stay, I can ask Zach—"

"It's fine. I'm just going to get rid of Ryan and then go inside and get a fire started. Call me later before you go to sleep?" Her expression was a mixture of hope and regret.

Rex knew exactly how she felt. He'd been planning on staying over again, but that was out now that his sister was in town. At least for the night. He needed to go visit her and find out the reason for her early arrival. "Of course. Call if you need anything, even if it's just to talk."

"I won't bother you and Amelia," she said and gave him a light kiss on the lips. "Go on now. Get her out of the cold. I'll talk to you later."

Rex nodded, but it was a struggle to force himself to move to his truck. He didn't want to leave Holly there was the presumptuous jackass. It wasn't that he didn't trust her or think that she couldn't handle the situation herself; it was that he wanted to be her support person when she told Ryan to get the hell off her property. Because judging by the stormy look on her face when she met the man's eyes, he certainly wasn't safe from her wrath. *Good*, Rex thought. It served him right.

Rex stared Ryan right in the eye and then leaned down and kissed Holly on the cheek. "I had fun tonight."

She smiled up at him. "So did I."

"Later." He squeezed her hand and then reluctantly returned to his truck, and for the first time in nearly a week, he headed home for the night.

CHAPTER 20

*H*olly stared after Rex's truck as the taillights faded into the night and wanted to scream at the man who was still standing at the base of her porch. The complete and utter shock of finding Ryan at her house waiting for her had nearly knocked her flat on her back. And had she heard that correctly? Had he really told Rex that she was his fiancée? The nerve.

"I think you should go," she said to Ryan as she brushed past him and up the stairs of her porch.

"Holly, please. I drove all the way here from New York. I'm back for good. Won't you just hear me out?"

"No." She shoved her key into the lock, praying that he would just go away. She was over Ryan. And she'd almost forgotten just how disarming his brooding good looks were. It wasn't as though she was going to get lost in his piercing blue eyes again. That reaction was long gone. But when he looked at her as if she was ripping his heart out, she couldn't help but feel something.

Dammit. That pissed her off. She blew out a long breath and opened her door.

"I brought you your tree," he said, his tone now light and almost teasing.

She turned around, rage boiling in her gut. "Do you really think a Christmas tree is going to make up for two years of desertion? You said you'd be back, Ryan! I believed you. I thought we were going to spend the rest of our lives together. But then that chickenshit letter showed up. Do you have any idea what that did to me?" She didn't wait for him to respond as she flew down the stairs, her arms outstretched in front of her. Just as she collided with him, knocking him off his feet, she cried, "I was *broken*, you jackass. *Broken.*"

It killed her to say the words out loud. To let him see just how much he'd hurt her. But she couldn't stop herself from unloading on him. How dare he act like he could walk in and out of her life with zero regard to her feelings.

"I'm with Rex now. You're too late," she said.

He stared up at her from his position on the ground, his mouth opening and closing as if he couldn't find the words to respond.

"Go back to wherever you were, Ryan. I'm not your future."

"You *are* my future," he blurted as he finally scrambled to his feet. "I thought I needed to prove myself first. That I needed to be at a certain level in my career before we got married and started a family. I just couldn't do that here in Christmas Grove. Please, Holly. Let me explain."

Start a family? The words hit her like a sucker-punch to the gut. It was the one thing she'd always wanted. Ryan knew that. They'd talked about it endlessly. Holly didn't have any family left, and she desperately wanted to create her own. She'd thought she and Ryan were on the same page. If they'd followed the blueprint she'd had for them, they'd already be married and she'd either have her first child or be pregnant at that moment. Unfortunately, Ryan had crushed those dreams when he walked away.

He'd left her, just like everyone else in her life. Even if she wanted to forgive him, to let him back into her life, she couldn't trust him now. She'd always be waiting for the next letter as he hightailed it out of town for something better than her and Christmas Grove.

Should she hear him out or just retreat back into her house? She couldn't deny that she was curious to hear what he had to say. Not that it would change her mind. She was sure of that. Besides, her heart was set on someone else now.

"If I let you talk, will you leave me alone?" she asked with her arms crossed over her chest.

"Holly," he said, shaking his head. "I'm not trying to harass you. I just want to have a conversation."

"Well, you are harassing me. You just showing up here like that... How do you think that made me feel? Huh? Do you think I wanted to bring my date home to this?" She waved a hand at the tree, hating that she felt a twinge of tenderness because he'd remembered something that she'd told him a long time ago. *Christmas trees are the easy part, Holly*, she told herself. *Don't fall for this.*

"Okay. Yeah, I can see how that didn't go exactly according to plan," he admitted, running a hand through his dark hair.

"What exactly was the plan, Ryan? Was I supposed to be so grateful that you decided to come back for me, *two years later*, and so overwhelmed by this tree that I flew into your arms and told you it was all okay now that you're back?" There was so much disdain in her tone she barely even recognized her own voice.

"No," he said slowly. "That's not... Listen, I made a huge mistake. All I want is a chance to make it up to you."

She nearly rolled her eyes. Instead she walked over to the porch swing and took a seat. While staring at the lit-up tree, she said, "Fine. I'm listening."

His footsteps sounded on the stairs and she knew he was coming to sit next to her, so she put her feet up into the swing, showing him that he wasn't welcome. If he wanted to talk, he'd have to do it while standing.

Ryan blew out a breath. "Okay, first off, I was wrong to let you know I wasn't coming back in a card. I should have called."

The irritation in Holly's gut only intensified. They'd been in a committed relationship. The jackass should've come home and talked to her in person. She continued to stare at the tree, her eyes burning from the sting of angry tears.

"I'm sorry, Holly. I was too scared to talk to you. I was afraid the moment I heard your voice I'd be on the next plane back here."

That got her attention. She turned her head to look up at him. "You're saying it hurt you to break things off with me? How badly? How long was it before you took another girl out? How exactly did you soothe your aching heart, Ryan?"

He winced at the accusation in her tone, and she knew right then and there that it hadn't been long at all. She'd waited two years. *Two years* before she'd let another man in her life. He'd probably waited two weeks.

"You are such an ass," she whispered.

He gave her a tiny nod. "I was. Definitely. You deserved better."

"You're damned right I did. And I still do." She jumped out of the swing and then ran past him down the porch stairs and straight to the tree. There was no way she could look at it for the rest of the season. All she'd see was red. Letting out a cry of frustration, she ran right into the tree, toppling it over. She fell on top of it with an *oomph* and immediately rolled off onto the cold earth.

"Holly! What the hell are you—" Ryan started.

"I'm getting rid of this monstrosity," she barked back as she grabbed the trunk and started pulling the tree toward the side of the house where she wouldn't have to see it. She'd get Rex or Zach to chop it up for the wood pile or something. But for now, she needed it out of her sightline. The tree was heavy. Almost too heavy for her smaller frame, but her adrenaline fueled her and finally, after much exertion, she managed to maneuver it along the side of her house. Sometime while she'd been dragging it, the lights had thankfully come unplugged.

She took a moment to stare at the tree carcass and then ran back up the stairs of her porch and pushed her way into her home, slamming the door behind her.

"Holly!" Ryan knocked on her door. "Come on. We can't leave it like this."

Holly let out a snort of pure aggravation before heading to the back of her house into the kitchen. Gods, she needed a hot mug of something. Preferably something spiked with a bit of alcohol. Her hands shook and were numb from the cold, but she managed to get the water into the coffee maker without spilling any. Once it was brewing, she moved to the refrigerator and retrieved the Irish Whiskey.

Ten minutes later, a mug of Irish coffee in one hand and a stack of Christmas cookies in the other, Holly made her way back to the front of her house. When she glanced out the window, she let out a small gasp as she watched snowflakes cover the tracks she'd made in her yard with the tree.

"Good. I won't have to look at the evidence in the morning," she said to herself.

Still peering out the window, she glanced over at the space where Ryan's truck was still parked. If he was trying to salvage that tree, she was going to lose it. But no, he wasn't. A flash of movement to the right drew her gaze, and that was where she spotted him. He was standing in front of one of her floor-to-ceiling windows, staring at his feet. He looked just as defeated as she'd felt two years ago.

In any other circumstance, it was likely his expression would've tugged at her heartstrings. Not tonight though. All she felt was numb.

Ryan lifted his head, stared her in the eye, and then nodded to the window. It had started to frost over, and it occurred to Holly it was the perfect holiday window. All it needed was some twinkling lights and—

Ryan pressed one finger to the glass and drew out a series of letters. When he was done, he mouthed, *I still love you.*

Her heart started to pound as she watched him walk to his truck, climb in, and then drive away.

A small sob escaped from the back of her throat as a dam of emotions crashed down on her. Everything she'd ever felt for Ryan came rushing back, along with all the pain he'd caused when he walked away so callously. Holly took a long sip of her coffee, felt the burn of the whiskey against the back of her throat, and then downed the rest. She was going to need a heck of a lot more where that came from if she was going to survive the night.

Because dammit, no matter how much she hated Ryan, that love she'd had for him was still there, too. And that was something she desperately didn't want to feel.

Holly longed to call Rex, to hear his voice. But he was with his sister and she didn't want to interrupt their time. So instead, she walked back into the dining room, retrieved Sabrina from her cage, and cuddled the bunny against her chest. Once she was settled on her green velvet couch, she pulled out her phone and pressed Ilsa's name.

"I thought you had a hot date with Rex?" Ilsa asked the moment she answered the call.

"It was interrupted. Can you come over? There's something I need to talk to you about," Holly said.

"What is it? Did Rex do something? Do I need to kick someone's ass?"

"Someone's, but it's not Rex," Holly said. "Ryan showed up tonight. He wants to pick up where we left off."

Ilsa was silent for more than a few beats. When she spoke again, she said, "I'm on my way."

CHAPTER 21

*R*ex jumped out of his truck and jogged over to his sister, who was sitting on his front porch bundled up in her down jacket and knit cap. If she hadn't looked so cold, she would've been adorable. His sister was a pixie with thick blond curls and large brown eyes. She was sweet, kind, and a totally fierce bitch when she needed to be. It was actually the thing he loved most about her. Most people thought she was too kind to call them on their crap. Rex knew differently.

"Come here," he said, opening his arms wide and waiting for her to jump into them like she always did when they were reunited. But she didn't. Instead, she pushed herself up on shaky legs and sort of wobbled over to him until she fell into his arms and held on with everything she had.

"Hey," he said softly, running his hand down her back. "What's wrong? What happened?"

"He's gone," she said through a muffled sob.

"Who's gone?" Rex searched his brain for the name of his sister's latest boyfriend but didn't come up with anyone. Last year she'd been dating a guy she'd met during a trip to Cape Cod, but that had been a short fling. Or at least that's what she'd told him. "Grayson? That guy from Massachusetts?"

"Yeah. He... I... we reconnected over the summer." She pulled back and wiped at her eyes. "We met on Cape Cod again."

"I see." Though he really didn't. It was unusual for her to not let him in on the details of her life. Why hadn't she told him they'd started back up?

"Stop looking at me like that," she said and waved to the door. "Let me in before my fingers freeze off, and then we can talk."

"Sure." He pulled his key out of his pocket and opened the door for her. Before he followed her in, he grabbed an armload of firewood. As he straightened, he took a deep breath and knew the snow was coming. He could always smell it. The clean, cold scent that was void of the trees growing all around them never failed him. If he had to guess, the snow would be there within the half hour.

It was a good thing he was home for the evening. Though he'd hated to leave Holly. He wanted to text her, to warn her about the snow, but he refrained. She had enough to deal with considering her ex was on her doorstep begging for another chance. He'd call her later after he heard about Grayson and how the bastard had gutted his sister.

Rex grabbed a few more pieces of wood that was stacked near the porch and then hurried into his warm cottage. He heard the water running in the bathroom as he got to work on building a fire in the fireplace.

Once the kindling seemed to be doing its job, Rex moved into the kitchen and pulled out a leftover lasagna and a bottle of red wine. Both were no doubt essential to get them through the evening.

By the time Amelia emerged from the bathroom, her freshly washed face was pink, and she'd ditched the knit hat, leaving her curls bouncing around her face. For a moment, she looked just as she had when she was fifteen.

"Jeez, Amelia, do you ever age? Your skin is glowing," he said.

She let out a humorless bark of laughter. "I bet it is."

"New skincare regimen?" He poured the wine into two glasses and noted how his sister's eyes tracked his movements.

But then she grimaced and pressed a hand to her abdomen. "Drinking isn't in the cards for me tonight," she said, looking pained. "My stomach is a little... out of sorts."

"Food poisoning?" he asked, wondering if he had anything that was blander than lasagna in his fridge.

"No. I don't think so. Just a little queasy after the flight. The lasagna smells good." She gave him a warm smile as she sat at the table, already reaching for the breadbasket.

He sat across from her and handed her the butter. "I probably have some ginger. I could juice some into some carrot juice if you think that would help the nausea."

She grimaced and shook her head. "Do me a favor and don't mention juicing vegetables while I'm getting ready to dig into this cheesy goodness, okay?"

He chuckled. "Okay. Just trying to look out for you."

Amelia gave him a grateful smile. "Thanks, big bro. Just being here is making everything better."

Rex dug into his lasagna, suddenly ravenous. His day had been long, and he hadn't even stopped for lunch. As he ate, he watched his sister. While her skin did appear to be glowing as if she was radiating from the inside out, there were also dark circles under her eyes, even though it was obvious she'd use a generous amount of concealer. He put his fork down and covered one of her hands with one of his own. After clearing his throat, he said, "You're not sleeping well."

She paused, the fork she was holding just inches from her mouth. "Why do you say that?"

"Amelia," he said with a sigh. "You look exhausted."

"I'm just tired after the trip."

He stared at her, holding her gaze until she was the one who glanced away. "You look like you haven't slept in a week, sis. It's not the kind of tired that comes from getting up too early and spending half the day on a plane. This looks bone-deep, and I'm worried."

She stared at her plate, and in a quiet voice, she said, "I already told you I'm upset because Grayson left."

"Okay. I get that. When did he leave?"

"Last week." She took a long sip of her water and grabbed another piece of bread.

"Are you going to tell me about that?" he asked gently.

Amelia didn't look up at him as she said, "He wasn't ready to commit."

"But you are? Didn't you say you two just reconnected this summer?" What was that, five or six months, tops?

She sighed again. "Rex... I don't want to talk about this."

"Yes, you do, otherwise you wouldn't have come here," he said keeping his tone light and free of judgement. "I know you better than anyone. You don't have to talk to me right now if you've changed your mind, but we both know you'll feel better when you get it out."

Tears filled her eyes and then ran unchecked down her cheeks. She waved a hand at her face. "This is why I didn't want to talk about it."

His heart felt like it was breaking in two as he got up and moved to her side of the table. He pulled a chair close, sat down, and wrapped his arms around her. "What happened, babe?"

"He... I..." She squeezed her eyes shut, and in barely a whisper, she forced out, "I'm pregnant."

Rex's entire body turned to ice as he processed the words. His sister was pregnant, and the father had left her? The ice turned to red-hot rage and he had to work to keep from tightening his grip on her arms. His insides were a jumble of emotions that he couldn't process. Shock, anger, sympathy, disgust... How could a man just up and leave a woman who was pregnant with his child? He couldn't comprehend it. Rex cleared his throat and tried for a calming presence. "You told him, and he left?"

She shook her head. "I haven't told him yet. I just found out yesterday." The tears flowed faster. "He left last week."

Rex pulled back and looked down at her. "He doesn't know." It wasn't a question.

"I called. He hasn't called me back."

"When? Yesterday?" he asked.

"This morning." She used her napkin to wipe at her eyes. "I asked him to call me back. Didn't want to tell him something like that through voice mail."

"That's probably smart." He sat back and slipped his fingers through hers, holding on to make sure she knew he supported her. "Why did he leave?"

Amelia looked up at him, her big eyes full of pain. "I told him I loved him. He wasn't ready to hear it."

He squeezed her hand harder and felt as if his own heart was shattering. "Oh, honey. I'm so sorry. I'm no substitute for the one you love, but I'm here no matter what. I'll take care of you and the baby. You know that, right?"

"Yes." Her voice was hoarse as if she was having trouble getting words out. "That's why I'm here. Sort of."

"Sort of?" he said with a small chuckle.

She hiccupped a laugh. "I needed to be near someone who loves me unconditionally. You're it. But I'm also in California for another reason."

"Is this where Grayson is?" he asked with a frown. He wasn't sure how he felt about that. If the guy ran just because she told him she loved him, then he definitely didn't deserve her. But there was a child involved now. He resolved to keep his opinion about the situation to himself. She needed to do what she needed to do.

"No." She picked up her fork and dug into her lasagna. After taking a bite, she turned to him again and added, "When Grayson left me last week, I just couldn't be in New York anymore. I needed a change, and I was talking to Yvette Townsend—"

"Jacob's wife?" Rex asked, surprised. "I didn't know you two knew each other."

"We met at a fire training seminar last year. She's a volunteer firefighter. Anyway, when we realized you and her husband are friends, we sort of hit it off and have been in touch. There's an opening for a fire fighter at the station in Keating Hollow, and she recommended me. Things moved quickly, and long story short, I'm moving there. I start just after Christmas."

Rex blinked at her, once again unable to process what she'd just said. "You're leaving New York?"

The tears filled her eyes again as she nodded. "I just really needed a change, Rex. Don't hate me. I know you took the

New York job partly because I was there. But let's face it. You won't be around much. Your company will be sending you all over the place and I'd... Well, I'd be stuck seeing Grayson everywhere, and I just can't do that. Not while I'm pregnant and trying to come to terms with being a single mom."

"I thought you said he left New York," Rex said.

"He did. I just meant I won't be able to escape the memories." She pushed the plate away from her and dropped her head down to the table. "I know I sound irrational. I just... I need a change." She turned her head so that she could see him, her eyes pleading with him for understanding. "Rex, I need support in this. Can you do that?"

Rex gently pulled his sister to sit upright and then led her over to the couch. He laid down and then patted the cushion, indicating she should lay down next to him. Once she was in place, he wrapped his arms around her and pressed a soft kiss to the top of her head. "Of course I'll support you, baby girl. You know that of all people, I completely understand the need to escape to a new place." But for the first time, as he spoke about the need to move on, there was a bitterness on the back of his tongue. And for once, he wasn't itching to leave yet. Christmas Grove was comfortable in a way that no other place had ever come close.

"Where did you go, big brother?" Amelia asked softly.

"Nowhere. I'm right where I'm supposed to be."

She sat up and eyed him suspiciously. "Do you mean here with me or here in Christmas Grove?"

He sat up, too, and started to answer that he meant with her. But the truth was he had a strange feeling that maybe she was right and he was supposed to be in Christmas Grove, too. He certainly felt like he was supposed to meet Holly. He had trouble imagining his life without her now.

"Oh. Em. Gee," Amelia said, pressing one hand to her mouth. "That woman you met here. She's got her hooks in you, doesn't she?"

"Hooks?" Rex rolled his eyes. "No, Amelia. Holly doesn't have hooks."

"But you're hooked on her. Holy... son of a... I can't believe it." Her eyes glinted, and that lightness she usually carried was back for the first time since she'd arrived. "My brother is in love."

"I am not," he insisted and ignored the voice in his head that called him a liar. "I just really like her... a lot."

Her lips twitched. "Like her. A lot. I see. When do I get to meet this Holly person? Is that who you were with when I called?"

"You can meet her tomorrow at dinner." His insides warmed with pleasure at the idea of introducing Holly to his sister. And wasn't that something? He hadn't introduced Amelia to anyone since Sara. That certainly meant something, didn't it? "Yes. I was with her. She's Zach's neighbor."

Amelia's eyebrows shot up as she glanced at the door. "I see. Were you planning to stay in tonight? Did I ruin any plans?"

The truth was, if Amelia hadn't shown up, there was no doubt he'd be with Holly at that very moment. If he wasn't already in her bed, he'd be finding a way to get her there even if it meant only curling up to watch another Christmas movie. He'd learned his girl was a sucker for a feel-good Christmas romance. But with her in his arms, he didn't care one bit what they watched. He was down, just as long as she was next to him, curled into his body. "No. You didn't ruin any plans."

"Yes, I did." She got up and paced, running a hand through her blond curls. "Dammit, Rex. I'm sorry. You can just leave me here. Go see her. I'll be fine."

He got to his feet and tugged her back down to the couch. "No. I'm staying here tonight with my sister, who I haven't seen in months, because I miss her and she needs me. I'll see Holly tomorrow, and you can grill her about why she's decided I don't bug her too much."

Amelia laughed. "I already know why. Because you're the best." She wrapped her arms around him and leaned her head against his shoulder. "Thank you for not judging me or freaking out."

"Judge you? About what? Being pregnant?" he asked, confused as to why she thought he'd judge her.

"Well, yeah. I guess."

He scoffed. "Honey, you're thirty-three years old. You make a fine living and will be the best mom. Honestly, other than your heartbreak about Grayson, I'm thrilled for you and can't wait to be an uncle. Only now I'm going to have to figure out how to get more jobs in Keating Hollow so I'm around a lot."

Tears filled her eyes again, but she was smiling up at him. "I love you."

"I love you, too, sweet girl. Now. Are you okay? Really okay? Losing your boyfriend, finding out you're going to be a mother, and taking a new job in a new city all in the same week is some major upheaval. I think I'd crawl into bed for a few days just to process it all."

"I actually might do just that," she said with a watery smile. "Now, where am I sleeping?" She patted the couch. "Here?"

He shook his head. "Nah. You take my room. I'll sleep on the couch."

"Rex, you don't have to—"

He held up a hand, cutting her off. "I know I don't have to. But you look exhausted, and you're a mommy-to-be now. I'm

167

allowed to spoil you. No arguments. The sheets are clean. I haven't slept here since I changed them a few days ago."

"Oh." Her grin widened. "I see."

"I bet you do." He pushed off the couch. "Now, help me with the dishes so we can enjoy this fire before we both pass out."

CHAPTER 22

$\mathcal{H}$olly woke with a start, and it took her a minute to realize it was the buzz of the phone that had startled her. When she saw Rex's name flash on the screen, she smiled. He wasn't even in her bed and he was still making an effort to make sure she didn't oversleep.

Rise and shine, gorgeous, the text said. *Get in the shower. I'm coming over to make you breakfast since we missed dinner last night. And I'm bringing my sister. Fair warning.*

Holly quickly tapped out her own message. *I'd love to meet your sister. I'm headed to the shower now. Let yourselves in and I'll meet you down there in thirty.*

I'll have the coffee ready.

Holly let out a tiny whimper of approval. He was the perfect man in every way except for the fact that he was leaving. She stumbled into her bathroom and ordered herself to stop thinking about his departure. It was going to mess up the time they did have together. And that was something she wasn't willing to sacrifice to her inevitable heartbreak.

"Live in the now," she ordered herself as she stepped under the warm spray.

When she finally entered the kitchen, she spotted the tiniest, cutest woman in dark jeans and a form-fitting red sweater, ordering Rex around.

"Just set the table. You know I'm better at omelets than you are. You always end up overcooking the eggs, leaving brown spots. You know how much I hate that."

"I do not overcook my omelets," Rex insisted. "It was just that one time when I was getting used to your electric stove."

"Move it, big bro. I'm starving, and it's faster if I just do it myself." She hip-checked him and poured the egg mixture into a waiting skillet.

"Good morning," Holly said from the doorway.

Rex turned and walked straight to her, wrapped an arm around her waist, and gave her a slow, lingering kiss on the lips. When he pulled back, his eyes were full of heat as he said, "Morning, gorgeous."

"Morning." She smiled into his beautiful blue eyes. "You're in a good mood. Is everything okay?" She inclined her head, indicating she was referring to his sister and her sudden appearance.

"Yeah. Everything will be fine." He glanced back at Amelia. "Just life stuff to work through." He brushed a lock of her hair out of her eyes and asked, "What about you? How did it go with Ryan last night?"

"I kicked him to the curb." She pressed a hand to his slightly stubbled jaw. "He's too late." The vision of Rex with a baby in his arms flashed in her mind, stealing some of the joy of her statement from her, but she pushed it aside. That was his future. She was his present.

"Good." Rex lowered his head and this time when he took

her mouth there was heat and need and possession that flipped all of her switches. If his sister hadn't been in the room, she was certain they'd have made their way to her bedroom to make up for their night apart.

"Oh. My. Goddess. You two need to get a room," Amelia said.

They broke apart, each of them giving each other a sheepish grin. She'd only said the words that all of them were thinking.

With a huge grin, Amelia said, "Don't mind me. I'll get myself fed and leave your omelets in the oven to keep them warm."

Holly put her hand on Rex's chest and gently pushed him back as she chuckled. "I love her already."

"Samesies," Amelia said with a wink. "Anyone that can put that look on my brother's face is A-ok in my book."

Holly moved to the coffee pot and poured some into her favorite mug. She turned to Amelia. "Did you need a cup?"

Amelia stared at the mug, a wistful expression on her face. "Um, yes, but only a half cup. I'm trying to cut down on my caffeine. Do you have milk?"

"Sure." After Holly poured a half cup of coffee, she grabbed the milk from the fridge. "How much?"

"Fill the cup up," Amelia said, turning back to the omelets to add avocado, tomatoes, and goat cheese—all were Holly's favorites.

"I'll do you one better." Holly reached up into her cabinet and pulled out an electric milk frother. In no time, the milk was heated and frothy when she poured it into the coffee mug.

Amelia took a sip and let out a sigh of pleasure. "You really are a saint." She glanced over her shoulder at her brother.

"Marry this one, okay? If you don't, I might snag her for myself."

Holly laughed, but when she glanced back at Rex, he was staring at her with an intensity she hadn't seen before. Their gazes met and held for a long moment, then Rex suddenly broke the connection and told Amelia, "Keep your hands to yourself, little sister. She's spoken for."

Amelia chuckled to herself. "Do you want bacon in yours?"

"Yes." He went to work on browning some toast while Holly set the table.

When they were all seated and digging into their breakfasts, Holly asked, "What do you two have planned for the day?"

Rex glanced at his sister. "I was going to start sorting the donated toys for the town Christmas celebration next week. Want to help?"

"You're in charge of the toy drive?" Amelia asked, her eyes full of surprise.

"Yep." He grinned at her. "And now since you've arrived early, you get to be my elf."

She groaned. "Just try not to boss me around. You know that never goes well."

The two of them bantered back and forth for the rest of the meal while Holly watched in fascinated silence. And maybe a little jealousy. She'd never had a sibling, so the dynamic was interesting to her. Sure, she had something close with Ilsa, but it wasn't the same. These two just looked like a team. Ride or die no matter what, both bound by blood, a shared youth, and genuine affection for each other.

Rex glanced over at her, his lips twitching into a small smile. "What is it, Hols? Are we amusing you?"

"Yes, actually. It's interesting to see you with your sister. You're lighter somehow. Freer, maybe."

"It's because I bring out the ten-year-old in him," Amelia said with a cackle. "He can't help himself."

Rex chuckled. "Isn't that the truth. You've been annoying me for thirty-three years now. And as much as I wished back when we were kids that you'd get a personality transplant, I think I've gotten used to you now. Just try to remember to keep my bathroom sink clean and we'll be all right."

She smirked. "As long as you remember to put the toilet seat down."

The way they both laughed, it was clear the exchange was one they'd had many times in the past. Holly's heart swelled with love for Rex and his sister. It made her happy to know he had her in his life.

After breakfast, Rex insisted on doing the dishes while Amelia followed Holly out onto her front porch. A light dusting of snow still clung to the ground from the night before, and the December air was that perfect blend of crisp snow and wood smoke from the neighboring houses.

"Thank you for the omelet," Holly said to her as she zipped up her jacket.

"Thank you for putting that dopey grin on my brother's face." Amelia had been smiling when she said it, but as she reached out to squeeze Holly's hand, her expression turned serious. "I know we just met, and I probably shouldn't be saying this, but I think you should know I've never seen Rex this happy."

Holly's insides lit up, and tears pricked her eyes as she said, "I feel the same actually. He's a great guy. I've never had anyone take care of me the way he does." As the words left her mouth, she frowned and added, "Not that I need anyone to take care of me. It just makes me feel like I mean something to him. And well, I don't think I've ever felt that before." Ryan certainly had never given her what Rex did.

Ryan had been a decent guy who'd been a lot of fun. But now that she thought about it, everything they did had to do with what interested Ryan—skiing, camping, movies, and even the concerts they'd gone to were always bands that he liked. Rex was completely different. So far, he'd proven to be a dream come true. Not only had he made the Great Hall happen, but he'd shown up at her baking class, taken her to her favorite restaurants, and jumped in to help the people of the town instead of always thinking about himself. And he liked to cook, so he'd been true to his word and made her dinner every night.

"What is Rex really passionate about?" Holly asked Amelia. "Besides his gift with earth magic I mean."

Amelia frowned. "I'm not sure what you're asking. Like a hobby?"

Holly shrugged. "Sure. Or just whatever interests him. I'm trying to figure out what to get him for Christmas, and I realized that I have no idea what kind of gift would be meaningful to him, except maybe books. I know he likes to read."

Amelia smiled and nodded her head. "That's a good one. If you can find him a signed copy of his favorite book, that would blow his mind." She pursed her lips and added, "Or something that has to do with photography. He takes the best photos. I keep telling him he should show his work, but he always ignores me."

"He's a photographer?" Holly blinked, feeling as if she'd been left out of something important. Rex had never mentioned anything about photography. Not even when she'd told him she liked to paint. Or had she? She searched through their many conversations and was surprised to realize she probably hadn't told him. Painting was something she did for herself to relax. Ever since she'd started spending time with Rex, she hadn't made time to paint anything. And just like that, she knew what to get him.

"Yep. He could probably make a career of it if he wanted to, but he says his photos are just for him. I'm actually not that surprised he hasn't told you. Don't take it personally. He didn't tell me either. I found him downloading shots to his computer one day at my house a few years ago. He tried to wave me off, but you can imagine how that went." She laughed at the memory. "They were gorgeous. It's too bad he won't try to do anything with them."

Holly knew for certain that she'd never seen Rex with a professional camera, and she wondered if, just like her, he'd put his hobby on hold while they spent time together. "Thanks for that," she said to Amelia. "It really helps."

"Sure." Then Amelia stepped forward and grabbed Holly into a fierce hug. As she pressed her cheek to Holly's, she whispered, "Whatever you do, don't let him go. He deserves you."

Holly stood frozen for a moment, hugging the other woman back. She couldn't make that promise. Holly knew better than to fight her visions. Rex was meant for some other woman. She gently untangled herself and said, "I'd like to hold on to him, Amelia, but I'm sure you know better than most that you can't hold someone back when all they want is freedom." She knew she sounded sad as she said the words. But she would not put herself in the same position she'd been in with Ryan. If Rex wanted to stay, she'd welcome him with everything she had. But when he left, as she knew he would, she'd let him go with love in her heart. She had to. Because she couldn't survive more broken promises. "He's a wanderer. We both know that," Holly added. "And, unfortunately, I'm not."

"He wasn't always," Amelia said with a tired sigh. "There was a time when all he wanted was a family."

"Then Sara happened," Holly supplied.

Amelia scowled. "That cow. She broke something in him that never healed. I'll never forgive her for that."

Holly gave the other woman a slight smile. "He's not broken. Just shaped by his experiences. So am I."

"Oh, hell." Amelia shook her head. "You really are perfect for him." Tears pooled in Amelia's eyes. "I just love him and want him to be happy."

"Me too." Holly gave her another quick hug and whispered, "I'm glad he has you." Then she escaped into her car and took off for work before she dissolved into her own puddle of tears.

CHAPTER 23

As the days passed, Rex, Holly, and Amelia fell into a routine. While Holly was at work, Rex and Amelia took care of everything related to the toy drive. They even went around town and picked up items the residents didn't have time to deliver to the Great Hall. And at night, Rex usually made dinner for the three of them. Holly and Amelia had become fast friends, making their evenings together easy and fun. There were a few nights when Amelia begged off to spend the evening alone in his cabin, leaving Rex and Holly to have a romantic evening together. On those nights they usually ended up having a bedroom picnic that ended with the food ignored.

Regardless of their dinner plans, Rex was back to staying at Holly's each night, letting his sister have his cabin. And although Amelia was certainly welcome for breakfast at Holly's, she rarely showed up due to her morning sickness.

"Is Amelia still not feeling well?" Holly asked Rex the morning of the Christmas ball.

"What? Who said she wasn't feeling well?" he asked as he poured batter into the waffle iron.

"She told me yesterday that she was a little queasy. I'm just wondering if she has a stomach bug or something."

Rex hadn't told Holly about Amelia's pregnancy. His sister had asked him not to say anything until she finally spoke with Grayson. He suspected she'd meant not to tell their family and that she probably hadn't been specifically talking about Holly, but he was respecting her wishes. If Amelia wanted Holly to know, surely she would've told Holly herself. "Oh, she's fine now," Rex said with a wave of his hand. "Nothing to worry about."

"That's good." Holly pulled a bowl of blueberries out of the fridge and placed them on the table. "She's coming to the ball tonight, right?"

"Definitely. She's been looking forward to it." He flipped the waffle onto a plate and handed it to Holly. "She got a dress yesterday and everything."

Holly set the plate on the counter and slipped her arms around his waist, hugging her chest to his back. "You're a good brother, you know that?"

Rex covered her entwined hands with one of his own and twisted his head to glance at her. "Why do you say that?"

"Because it's true. She's going through a rough breakup, and you're here for her to lean on. You're helping her move next week, taking care of everything so that she doesn't have to stress over it. You're her brother, but you're also her best friend. It's pretty wonderful, actually."

"She told you about Grayson?" he asked, wondering what else they'd talked about.

"Yeah. A few days ago." Holly rested her head against his back and let out a soft sigh. "I heard her leaving him a message.

She was pretty upset, so when I asked what was wrong, it just kind of all came spilling out. Since I have some experience with someone I loved leaving me behind, it was easy to relate."

Rex stiffened at the mention of her relationship with Ryan. They hadn't talked about him since the morning after he'd surprised her with the giant tree that was still laying along the side of her house. And since Holly and Rex had spent every night together since then, he knew Ryan wasn't in her life, but he still felt the need to ask about the man. He was still in town, after all. "Have you seen Ryan since that night?"

She let out a slow breath. "Yes."

Rex poured more batter into the waffle iron and then turned to face her. "How did that go?"

Her expression was pinched, and it was clear she didn't want to talk about her ex, but she met his eyes anyway and said, "He's convinced we're going to get back together eventually. Says he's here for good and not going anywhere this time. I keep telling him it's too late, but he just nods, says he hears me, but still isn't giving up. Honestly, he's exhausting."

Rex's gut clenched as he thought of the other man courting his girl once Rex left town. The idea made him both angry and sick to his stomach. Holly wouldn't have any reason to not give him another chance. Other than her own trust issues, of course. But Rex would be gone, and they'd already said they'd let each other go.

Only with each passing day it was becoming clearer and clearer that he didn't want to let her go. He wanted to tell her that even when he left, he'd always come back. But she'd been down that road before, and the idea of saying that to her seemed ludicrous.

"What if he is back for good?" he heard himself ask and then cringed. What the hell was he doing?

179

She turned and stared at him. "What do you mean by that?"

He shrugged. "If he is back for good, maybe you should think about forgiving him. You did love the guy once, right?"

Her confused expression turned downright incredulous as she stared at him open-mouthed. "You think I should *forgive* him?"

That was clearly the wrong thing to say. And if he was honest, it soothed him to know she was in no mood to take the guy back. "No," he said slowly, taking care with his words. "I don't think you *should* do anything. I was just suggesting that if you loved him, maybe there is room for forgiveness and a possible future."

"Is that how you feel about Sara?" she asked, her voice flat as if she were void of any emotion. "If she showed up here today, all apologetic and begging for another chance, would you be so open to giving it another go?"

Oh, hell. He'd really stepped in it this time. "No. What Sara did... It's not worthy of forgiveness."

"And what Ryan did is? Is this because you're feeling guilty for getting close to me and then leaving? Are you trying to soothe your own conscience? Because if so, just butt out, Rex. I don't need you telling me how I'm supposed to feel. Not about Ryan and not about you when you eventually walk out of my life." She turned on her heel and stormed out of the room.

"Holly! Wait, I—"

The front door slammed, cutting him off.

"Son of a..."

"You're an idiot." His sister's voice came from the back of the house.

Rex jerked his head up and met his sister's eyes. She was standing just inside the back door, shaking her head at him. "How much of that did you hear?"

"Enough to know you were trying to push her to take Ryan back even though it's obvious she's in love with you." She tsked and walked over to him to grab the ignored waffle Holly had left on the counter. "When are you going to let go of your fear of commitment and finally let yourself be happy, big brother?"

"I don't fear commitment." The lie was sour on his tongue.

"Sure you don't." She drizzled syrup on the waffle and moved over to the table. "You're on the verge of losing her. You know that, right? And you're going to regret it for the rest of your life."

"Amelia," he said, a warning in his tone. "Just stop. Please."

"Nope. I don't think I will." She gave him a bratty smile and then dug into the waffle. After she swallowed, she added, "I'm just telling you what you need to hear." Then she sobered. "You need to go after her."

"I think she wants her space," he said, crossing his arms over his chest. The nagging voice inside his head said that his sister was right, though. Holly needed to hear that he didn't want her back with her ex. That it was killing him that he was leaving in two weeks. He knew that he'd probably brought up Ryan as a way to protect himself. If he believed that she and Ryan were supposed to be together, it would be the perfect excuse for him to leave and not look back. To keep living his life the way he had for the last ten years. No commitments, no problems.

He liked that life. It was easy.

"You need her," Amelia said.

"I needed you to stay in New York," he snapped.

There was silence in the kitchen as his words echoed off the walls.

Finally, Amelia turned her attention back to the waffle and said, "I see. After all these years of me always supporting you, defending you to Mom, and dropping everything to see you according to your schedule, now that I need something for me, it's inconvenient for you. Well done, big brother, you've managed to piss off the two women you love most." She stood and took her plate to the sink. "Happy now?"

"No." He couldn't remember a time when he'd felt as gutted. He knew he was being an ass, and yet, he couldn't bring himself to face the reasons why. "I'm sorry, sis."

"I'm sure you are." She pressed a hand to his cheek and focused on him, her brown eyes peering into his baby blue ones. "You need to figure out what you really want and then fight for it or else you're never going to be whole."

He nodded because he knew she was right. He just didn't know if he could stay in one place. And ultimately, if he wanted Holly, he'd have to stay in Christmas Grove for the long haul. Could he do that? He hadn't been able to stay in one place for longer than a handful of months for the past ten years. The idea was daunting and seemed impossible. He just didn't know if he was capable of that much change. He didn't want to make promises to Holly if he wasn't sure he could keep them.

"I need to take a walk," he told his sister.

"Sure." She glanced at the sink. "I'll clean up and then go back to the cabin."

"Thanks." He bent his head and kissed her on the cheek. "I'm sorry about what I said."

"I know." She swatted him on the arm. "Now go find her."

CHAPTER 24

*H*olly didn't have any idea where she was going when she stormed out of her house. She hadn't even brought her keys, so taking a drive was out of the question. She had remembered to grab her coat off the rack next to the door, however. And for that she was grateful. The mornings were always cold this time of year.

She walked down her driveway through another light dusting of snow. It was just as pretty as it had been the week before, but she didn't find any joy in it. She was too busy being pissed off at Rex. How dare he try to tell her how she should feel about Ryan? And more importantly, why was he pushing her to forgive her ex?

Had she been right when she'd accused him of feeling guilty for getting close to her and then leaving? Did he think it would be easier for her if she had Ryan waiting in the wings? The very idea of Rex trying to push her into Ryan's arms made her nauseated. It wasn't because she was still angry at Ryan or even that Rex was wrong about Ryan deserving another chance. If he moved to Christmas Grove and put down roots, maybe he did. She didn't know.

What she did know was that she'd fallen in love with Rex and the idea of him with another woman made her sick to her stomach. Every time she recalled her vision and saw him with his newborn, she wanted to burst into tears. She had to admit that she wanted to beg him to stay in Christmas Grove, to stay with her, to love her enough that there was no other option. She deserved that, didn't she? She deserved to be put first for a change, right?

The thought of asking someone to put her before their career or their preferred lifestyle seemed incredibly selfish. Shouldn't she be willing to make the same sacrifice? If she truly loved Rex, shouldn't she be willing to give up Christmas Grove and travel with him to his various jobs? Holly wasn't sure when the idea had first formed, but it was true that she was entertaining the thought. She'd even convinced herself to bring it up to Rex. But then he'd gone and told her to reconcile with her ex. Clearly, he wasn't interested in turning their short affair into a long-term thing. And that was the real reason she was so upset.

Holly found herself standing in front of the Great Hall. The magical decorations were just as impressive as they had been the day Rex had helped put it all together. In the past few weeks, most of the town had brought their kids to be sorted or to drop off presents. Even now, there were toys on the drop off table after they'd cleared it the night before. The toy drive had been a massive success by anyone's measure, and there was no doubt Rex deserved all the credit. He'd made sure everyone knew where to go, the ages of the kids they needed toys for, and he'd even put together a wish list based on the kids who needed the most help.

Her eyes burned with tears as she made her way into the hall and toward the front to admire the giant tree. It was magnificent. Even larger than the one Ryan had tried to use to win her over last week. It was likely the largest one Zach had sold all season. She smiled as she gazed up at it and started to feel some of the anger ease from her chest.

Holly was angry at Rex, hurt even that he didn't seem willing to change his life for her. But she'd given no indication that she'd change hers for him either, so maybe he thought they were both on the same page. Could she really fault him for that? As far as he knew, she was in Christmas Grove for good. She let out a long sigh. What a mess.

"Is this seat taken?" Rex's gruff voice sounded behind her.

Holly glanced back at the gorgeous man and gave him a faint smile. "Looks like it's free."

Without a word, Rex sat beside her and took her hand in both of his. "I'm sorry."

"For?" she asked, genuinely curious to hear his answer.

"For trying to tell you how you should feel. That wasn't my place."

No. It wasn't. "I appreciate that."

"Sure."

An awkward silence fell between them, and Holly knew they both had things to say that neither knew how to express. She could either stay silent and pretend nothing was wrong or put her heart on the line and live her life with no regrets. Saying nothing was the easy way out. She already knew the outcome. Her vision had made sure of that. But there was still a nagging voice deep inside of her that demanded she tell this man how she felt. If she didn't, she was going to be the one with regrets. "Is there any..." She swallowed hard. "Do you think there's any chance of us continuing this relationship after you leave for New York?"

Rex turned to her, his expression full of regret.

She closed her eyes and turned away. "Never mind. I just… I really like you. More than I should."

Rex placed his hand over hers and squeezed. "I think I'd love nothing more than to continue what we have. But how would that work with us living three thousand miles apart? Plus, I'd be traveling all over for work. It would be hard for me to get back here."

Her heart soared with the confirmation that Rex wanted something more with her. But it plummeted just as fast when she realized he'd already thought about the logistics and obviously dismissed the idea. "I guess I was thinking that we could just see where this goes and if we decide to take it further. We don't have to live in Christmas Grove. I'd be willing to consider New York or somewhere else."

Rex tightened his hold on her hand as he let out a slow breath. "I don't want to ask you to do that."

"You didn't ask," she said, staring straight ahead at the giant tree. "I offered."

There was more silence, and Holly knew this conversation was going nowhere. After a few beats, she gently untangled her hand from his and got to her feet. Refusing to be a chicken, she looked him in the eye and said, "It's okay, Rex. I understand. We always said this was temporary. There's no need to change it now."

"Hols," he said. But then he just closed his eyes and shook his head as he muttered, "I'm sorry."

"There's no need to be." She touched his face, lightly trailing her fingertips over his jawline. "I understand. You're a traveler and I'm not. It's not fair of me to try to change you, just like it's not fair of you to try to tell me how I should feel about Ryan."

He opened his eyes with a start. "That's not..." Shaking his head, he said, "I just want you to be happy, Holly. It actually kills me to think of you with that guy." He tugged her closer, gently guiding her down onto his lap. "If you haven't noticed, I'm crazy about you. It's killing me that I'm going to have to leave in two weeks. And a part of me wants to beg you to go with me."

"Why don't you?" she asked, hating that there was so much emotion in her voice. She didn't want him to know exactly how much it hurt that he didn't want her as much as she wanted him.

"Because it isn't fair to you. Like I said before, even though my job is in New York, I'm going to be traveling all over the country and internationally. How do you think that would work, with you waiting for me back in New York, always waiting for that phone call?"

He didn't have to say what phone call he was referring to. He meant the first responder who would call when his plane went down. It made no difference that statistically there was nothing to worry about. It only mattered that she'd received that call before and she'd relive it over and over and over again each time he traveled for one of his jobs. She couldn't hold back the tears. "You're right," she said on a small sob. "I couldn't live that way. And I can't ask you to not travel for your job. So even if I did move, we're still back to where we started. Just a holiday fling and then we part ways as friends, right?"

"Holly," he said, running one hand through her loose locks. "We will always be more than just friends."

"Sure." And even though she felt like her heart had just shattered into a million pieces, she leaned in and kissed him.

His arms wrapped around her, holding her tightly as he deepened the kiss. There was desperation in the air, as if neither of them ever wanted to let the other go. When Holly finally broke the kiss and buried her head in his shoulder, they sat there a long time, just holding onto each other.

"I think I'm going to regret leaving Christmas Grove," Rex said.

She pulled back and stared up at him, not caring that her face was likely splotchy from her tears. "Are you sure it's Christmas Grove you're going to regret leaving?"

He shook his head. "No. I'm certain it's *who* I'm leaving that will keep me up at night."

She let out a slow breath. "Good."

Rex chuckled and kissed her temple. "You're something else, Holly Reineer. You know that, right?"

She didn't know how to answer him, so she just nodded and said, "Come on. Let's go back to the house. I want to spend some private time with you before we go to the ball tonight."

Heat flashed in his gorgeous blue eyes as he nodded and silently followed her back into the house.

CHAPTER 25

*R*ex stood in Holly's living room waiting for his girl and his sister to emerge from upstairs. After spending most of the day with Holly in his arms, he'd reluctantly gotten up and headed back to his cabin to dress for the ball. Now he was back, sporting a black suit with a tie that the salesperson said matched his eyes. But all he really wanted to do was spend a quiet night with Holly.

Their fight earlier in the day had left him feeling as if a hole had been drilled through his heart. He knew he was the one that rejected her idea of them continuing their relationship, but he'd done it out of concern for her, despite the fact that it had nearly killed him. He wanted her more than he wanted his next breath. He just didn't know what to do with that.

Steps sounded on the stairs, and he glanced up to see his sister smiling down at him. Her blond hair had been pulled up into a half bun with curls framing her face. Her pregnancy was still in the early stages, giving off no hints of her condition. She wore a bright red dress that accented her curves and had a slit that showed off plenty of thigh. "Damn, Amelia. You look fantastic. Though as your brother, I feel it's probably my duty to tell you to cover up a little more."

Amelia glanced down at herself and laughed. "No way, dude. If I'm gonna be carrying around a basketball in a few short months, I'm gonna show off what I have while I can." She grinned at him as she strode over to where he stood and pointed at one of the roses he'd picked up from the florist a few hours ago. "Is one of those for me?"

"Yep." He picked up the red one that had already been clipped and tucked it behind one of her ears.

She grinned and quickly secured it with some sort of hair clip. "It's perfect. Thanks for remembering."

He nodded. For as far back as he could remember, his sister had always worn a flower in her hair when she got dressed up for parties. It was sort of her signature thing.

The sound of heels on hardwood drew Rex's attention to the top of stairs.

Holly grinned down at him, and the sight of her nearly took his breath away. He was certain he'd never seen anyone more beautiful. She stood there in a gorgeous shimmering silver dress, her red hair straightened and pulled up into a fancy twist that made her look like a movie star. He sucked in a sharp breath and moved forward to meet her as she made her way down to the bottom step.

Rex held out his hand, took hers and kissed her palm softly. "You're gorgeous."

She flashed him a brilliant smile and said, "So are you."

He scoffed when he looked down at himself. "Every guy in the place will be wearing the same thing. But you... You're going to take everyone's breath away."

"That's what I told her," Amelia said from behind them. She

grabbed the long-stemmed white rose Rex had gotten for Holly and handed it to him.

"Thanks, sis." Rex fixed his gaze on his girl and said, "This is for you."

Her grin widened. "Romantic. Thank you." Holly's gaze shifted to Amelia. "That rose looks fantastic there."

Amelia brushed her fingertips over the petals and said, "Thanks."

"Let me put this in water and say goodnight to Sabrina, and then we can go." Holly strode into the kitchen, leaving Rex to gape after her.

"Close your mouth, big brother. You're going to start drooling at any moment."

Rex laughed. "Start? You're giving me a lot of credit. I'm fairly certain I've left a puddle of drool on the floor already."

Chuckling, Amelia made her way to the door. "I'll go get the truck warmed up. Try to keep your pants on, will ya? I'm really looking forward to this party."

Rex flipped her off as she slipped her coat on and disappeared outside.

Holly reemerged from the kitchen, her lips curled up into a tiny smile. "Sabrina is all tucked in and happy with a couple of extra carrots."

"That's good." Rex pulled her coat off the coat rack and held it up so she could slip it on.

"You're being quite the considerate date. First a rose, and now this?" She kissed him on the cheek before turning around and letting him help her with her coat.

"You're stunning," he said, hearing the reverence in his own voice.

Her face flushed pink and he thought he'd never seen

anything prettier. "Come here." He tugged her in close to him and brushed a kiss over her nose.

"Did I leave you unsatisfied this afternoon?" she teased.

"Hell no," he said with a slight shake of his head. "I just can't keep my hands off you."

Holly practically melted into him, and Rex decided his sister had been right to warn him to keep his pants on. One word from Holly and he'd be carrying her back upstairs.

"We're going to be late if you keep looking at me like that," Holly whispered.

The sound of her sweet voice just did things to him. "Is that a bad thing?"

"Your sister might get annoyed."

"Right." He smirked, grabbed her hand, and led her outside to the truck.

"I'm impressed," Amelia said from the back seat. "I was certain it would take at least fifteen minutes to—"

"Amelia," Rex warned. "Shut it."

She cackled and said, "Sorry, Hols. He's just too easy a target."

Holly turned and grinned at Amelia. "I like when you fluster him. It's cute and makes him more human."

"See that, Rex? Your girlfriend likes when I poke the bear."

Rex felt a surge of pleasure at the idea that Holly was his girlfriend. He'd been calling her his girl all this time, but that was the first time anyone else had referred to her as his girlfriend, and he decided he liked it. Very much. He glanced over at the woman in question and met her gaze just for a second before he winked and turned his attention back to the road.

The Christmas ball, which was held outside in the middle of the town square, turned out to be a winter wonderland. The town of Christmas Grove had gone all out, creating a space that sparkled with thousands of lights, magical floating snowflakes, animated ice sculptures, and even a winter queen who could magically conjure champagne out of thin air.

"Wow," Amelia said as they made their way toward the buffet line. "It's not even cold here."

"There's a bunch of outdoor heaters, but also, all of the chairs at the tables are heated, so no one gets a cold tush." Holly nodded to Lemon, who was wearing the most gorgeous yellow chiffon dress. "She's our most talented air witch. I'm sure the town employed her to cast a spell to keep the heat from filtering out of the square."

"My town back home never did anything like this," she said reverently. "Maybe I should've chosen Christmas Grove over Keating Hollow."

"No way!" a female voice called from behind them. "I didn't work all these weeks to get you to Keating Hollow just to have you seduced by a really good party."

Rex turned and grinned at his friend's wife, Yvette Townsend. Jacob, one of his college friends was right behind her as they made their way to Rex, Holly, and Amelia.

"Yvette?" Amelia asked. "Is that you?"

"It is. Don't I clean up nice?"

Amelia laughed. "Yes, you do." The two of them hugged while Rex leaned in and gave Jacob a bro hug.

"Hey, man. I didn't know you two were going to be here," Rex said to Jacob.

The tall, dark-haired man nodded to his wife. "She just told me yesterday we were making the trip over. Shannon and Brian are here somewhere, too. Probably making out behind the Christmas tree. Ever since they got engaged, they can't seem to keep their hands off each other."

"I heard that," Brian said, appearing from behind the Christmas tree just as Jacob had guessed. He had red lipstick on his cheek and was slightly wrinkled.

"Holy hell, man. Look at you. Couldn't you wait until you got back to the hotel tonight?" Jacob chastised.

Brian shrugged, obviously not giving a damn what anyone thought. "Have you seen Shannon? No man in his right mind would turn down her advances."

A gorgeous woman who was all curves with thick, dark red hair glided over to them. She was wearing a green corset dress that showed off all her best assets. And while her fiancé was disheveled, she didn't have a hair out of place. She took one look at Brian and burst out laughing. "You look like you just had a quickie under the Christmas tree."

"Didn't he?" Jacob asked with one raised eyebrow.

She threw her head back and laughed. "No, but that could've been fun." She snickered and then added, "Brian dropped a cufflink and then had to crawl around under the tree to get it." Eyeing the lipstick on his face, she reached over and wiped it off.

Brian shrugged one shoulder. "My story was more entertaining."

Rex grinned at all of them, not realizing how much he'd missed them over the past month. Damn, it felt nice to be surrounded by them again. He draped an arm around Holly's shoulders and pulled her in close. "Guys, there's someone I want you to meet. This is Holly Reineer, my date."

The four of them turned to take in Holly.

Brian let out a whistle, resulting in an elbow to the gut by his fiancée. "Oomph," he said, side-eyeing her. "I was just paying Holly a compliment. Look at her. She's way too pretty for Rex's ugly mug."

Rex chuckled. "He's not wrong."

"Um, thanks?" Holly said and everyone laughed.

After the laughter died down, Rex added, "She's a talented baker, and if you stop by Charming Cookie's, you might be able to grab some of her Christmas cookies before you hightail it back to Keating Hollow."

"Thanks," Holly whispered in his ear. They'd spent part of the week before supplying the bakery with Holly's cookies after Cookie Kelly requested some to sell for the holidays.

"Sure, babe." He pulled her closer and pressed a kiss to her cheek. When he glanced back at his friends, both Jacob and Brian were staring at him, their eyebrows raised and their mouths hanging open. "What?"

"You've got a girl," Brian said and nodded in approval. "It's about time, man."

"No kidding. How long has it been?" Jacob asked. "Ten years?"

Holly laughed and moved away to go talk to Yvette, Shannon, and Amelia. She waved and mouthed, *Good luck,* as she followed the women to the buffet table.

"It has not been ten years since I dated," Rex insisted to his friends.

"Dated. But it's the first time you've had a girlfriend," Brian said.

"She's not..." Rex suddenly realized he couldn't finish that sentence. The fact was, he did think of Holly as his girlfriend and calling her anything else felt wrong.

Jacob laughed. "It's okay, man. We understand. We've both been there when the brain stops working and everything you thought was true turns out to be utter crap." He glanced over to the buffet table at the women. "She's gorgeous, Rex. And seems to like you. Hold on to that one, or you'll regret it."

"You have no idea," Rex muttered.

"Don't I, though?" Jacob waved the ball's Christmas queen over and ordered three glasses of champagne. After she produced them all just by snapping her fingers, Jacob raised his glass in a toast. "To love and finding your person."

Brian raised his glass and repeated the toast while Rex eyed Holly. Was she his person? His heart sped up and his mouth went dry. He wasn't sure how to interpret that reaction, but he was pretty sure it meant yes.

"Rex?" Jacob prompted.

"Huh?" He still had his eyes on Holly, remembering what it felt like to touch her smooth skin earlier that day.

"You're leaving us hanging here," Jacob said.

He jerked his attention back to his friends, coughed, and said, "Sorry." After raising his glass, he repeated the toast. "To finding your person."

The three of them clinked glasses and then downed the bubbly liquid. Rex set his glass down. "I don't know about you two, but there's a woman over there that I need to get on the dance floor."

"Dance floor, right," Brian said with a snicker. Then he called, "Use protection."

Rex ignored him and went to find his girl.

The night was pure magic. Rex kept Holly in his arms for most of the next two hours and was just about to take her home to reenact the afternoon they'd spent in her bed when there was a commotion near the Christmas tree.

"Rex!" He heard Yvette calling to him. "It's Amelia!"

"Amelia?" Holly cried, and they both took off to find Rex's sister flat on her back, her face as white as the magical snowflakes filling the room.

"Hey, sis," Rex said, kneeling beside her. "Wake up, now.

Open your eyes." He heard someone say an ambulance was on its way, and while he was grateful, he was also unable to breathe. "I need you to open your eyes," he said while he gently trailed his fingers over her forehead. He could see her chest rising with each breath she took, so he knew she was breathing. But he didn't know why she'd passed out. A bit of his magic might help jolt her awake, but since he knew she was pregnant, he didn't want to mess around.

"Excuse me. Healer coming through."

Rex glanced up to find Healer Harrison pushing her way through the crowd. The tall blonde was all business, and when she dropped down on the other side of Amelia, she gave no care for the white silk dress she was wearing.

"What happened?" the healer asked him.

"I don't know. She passed out I guess."

"I can see that," she said briskly. "Any reason why that might be? Did she eat today? Any signs of a virus or cold that could be wearing her down?"

"She's pregnant. A few months, I think," he said.

"Okay. That might explain a few things." She placed her hand on Amelia's forehead and then ran her hand down to her pulse.

Amelia's eyes fluttered open and she glanced around, clearly confused. "Rex?"

"I'm right here, sis. It's okay. You just passed out."

Amelia groaned. "I knew I'd cinched my waist too tight."

Healer Harrison clucked her tongue at Amelia. "What were you thinking, young lady? In your condition that's always a recipe for disaster."

Amelia groaned again and turned her gaze on Rex. "You told her about the baby?"

"What else was I supposed to do? You passed out!"

"Right. Sorry. I'm just..." She tried to push herself up, but Healer Harrison put a palm on her chest and nudged her back down.

"Just relax while I catalog your vitals," the healer said.

Rex studied her, wondering how exactly she was taking Amelia's vitals. The healer had her fingers on Amelia's neck, and her thumb and forefinger around her wrist. There wasn't anything that indicated she was taking her temperature or checking her eyes. But he supposed the healer could probably sense things he couldn't and told himself to relax.

Sirens sounded in the distance, and Healer Harrison ordered everyone to move out of the way, to give Amelia space. She glanced up at Rex. "I'm going to have them take her to my office. Is that okay with you?"

He glanced at Holly, who had one arm wrapped around her middle and the other her chest. "The healer's clinic or somewhere else?"

"Healer Harrison's clinic," she said.

He gave the healer a quick nod and turned his attention back to his sister. It wasn't long before he was climbing into his truck, ready to follow the healer to her office. Holly stood at his window. "Do you want me to go with you?"

"Yes, but it's probably better for you if you don't. I imagine I'll be by Amelia's side most of the night, and..."

"I'd be in the waiting room. I get it. I'll get a ride home from someone. Don't worry about me."

He reached through the window and cupped her cheek. "I'm sorry the night ended on such a bad note. I had a wonderful time with you."

"So did I. There's no need to be sorry." She leaned in and gave him a quick kiss. "Now go. Be there for your sister. You know where to find me."

"I'll come by your house after we get back to the cabin." He brushed his fingers over her smooth cheek and felt the words *I love you* on the tip of his tongue. But he swallowed them. Now was not the time for declarations. "Get some sleep. I'll come see you as soon as I can."

Then he put the truck in gear and rushed to the clinic.

olly found Ilsa waiting for her near the entrance when she stepped back into the square.

"Is Amelia okay?" Ilsa asked.

"I think so. The healer said she passed out because her waist cincher was too tight. I guess she just found out she's pregnant." Holly glanced around at the party that was still in full swing. "Listen, I'm just going to go home. Now that Rex is gone, I don't feel like being here. I'll get a carriage or something."

"Nonsense. Zach and I are giving you a ride home." Ilsa nodded to Zach, who was talking to Lemon a few feet away.

"You really don't have to do that. I don't want to ruin your night, too." She started to pull away from Ilsa, but her friend reached out and grabbed her hand, stopping her.

"Who says you're ruining my night? Zach and I are ready to leave anyway." There was a shy smile on Ilsa's face that had Holly narrowing her eyes in suspicion.

"So… the date is going well, then?" Holly asked.

Ilsa's lips curved up into a secretive smile. "Very well. He asked me to come back to his place."

"Finally!" Holly said in a loud whisper.

When Zach and Lemon both turned to look at them, Ilsa and Holly laughed.

"Come on," Ilsa said. "Let's rescue my date and get out of here."

Holly followed Ilsa, admiring her friend's long dark hair and the way her sleek ponytail hung perfectly down her back. She was wearing the red dress and silver shoes they'd picked out the day they'd gone shopping, and Holly thought Ilsa had never looked better. "You're hot in that dress."

"Yes, she is," Zach said, eyeing his date from head to toe.

Ilsa flushed as she took his hand in hers. "Thanks, Zach. That's sweet of you to say." She cut her gaze to Lemon. "Sorry to cut the conversation short, but Zach is our ride."

Lemon puckered her lips at Ilsa as if she'd just sucked on something sour and then cut her gaze to Holly. "I thought you'd be with your boyfriend and his sister."

Boyfriend. A lot of people had called Rex her boyfriend that evening. She hadn't had the heart to correct any of them. And she wasn't going to start now. "They are with Healer Harrison. I'll see them in the morning."

Before Lemon could ask anything else, Ilsa took Holly by the hand and started to tug her toward the parking area outside of the square. Zach was right on their heels, jingling his keys in one hand.

"Wow, when did Lemon turn into such a catty bird?" Zach asked when they reached his Tahoe SUV.

"I'd say the moment she decided you're interested in Ilsa," Holly said.

"Why? Does Lemon have a thing for my date?" Zach open the passenger doors for both Ilsa and Holly.

Ilsa snorted. "Hardly. She has a thing for mine."

"What?" Zach asked, clearly taken aback.

"Oh, honey," Ilsa said with a chuckle. "You're so blind. Lemon has had a crush on you for years."

"No, she hasn't," he said quickly and then frowned. "You're being serious, aren't you?"

Ilsa nodded and then turned to Holly for confirmation.

"Yep. She's had it bad for as long as I can remember," Holly confirmed.

Zach ran a hand through his thick dark hair. "Wow. I never realized."

Ilsa patted his hand. "We know." Then she climbed into the Tahoe. Holly did the same and rested her head back against the seat, suddenly bone tired. It had been one heck of a long day. Enjoyable sure. Or had been right up until Amelia passed out. But now she was spent, and all she wanted was to fall into bed.

Unfortunately for Holly, heading straight to bed the moment she got home was not an option. Zach and Ilsa had already dropped her off and were retreating back down the driveway when she noticed Ryan sitting in her porch swing holding a bouquet of sunflowers.

She bit back a curse. What was he doing there?

"Hi, Holly. Wow. You look incredible." He got to his feet as she climbed the porch stairs.

"What are you doing here, Ryan?" she asked in a tired voice.

He shoved his hands in his pockets and took a step closer. "I needed to talk to you. And I wanted to do it today."

"Why? Did you hear Rex wouldn't be here?" she barked out and unlocked her door, pushing it open.

"No." He frowned as if her question confused him. "Honestly, I thought he'd be with you. Did something happen?"

Holly stared at him as if he had two heads. "You're kidding me, right? You mean you were just waiting for me here on my porch, fully expecting Rex to bring me home. Didn't you think that would be awkward?"

"Yes," he said bluntly. "But I had to talk to you today. It's the day I told you I'd be back two years ago."

Holly bit down on her bottom lip and tried to recall the date on the calendar. If she was correct, it was six days until Christmas. December nineteenth. The day Ryan was supposed to propose to her. She got lost in her thoughts as she recalled the year before and how she'd stayed in bed all day, crying her eyes out and eating ice cream straight from the container. Then she barked out a laugh as she remembered that she'd also spent the day in bed this year, only she hadn't been crying or eating ice cream.

"Holly?" Ryan said, pulling her out of a particularly delicious memory.

"Huh?" she said, blinking at him.

"Do you think we could go inside. The snow is really starting to fall now."

She spun around and let out a tiny gasp. Big, fluffy flakes of snow had started to fall, and they were coming fast and furious. If it kept it up, the roads would be impassable in no time. "You should probably go, Ryan. You don't want to get stuck here."

He cleared his throat. "Um, it's too late already."

She closed her eyes and wanted to scream. "What does that mean?"

"I took my truck in to get serviced. It wasn't ready to pick up, so I had PJ drop me off."

PJ was a friend of his from high school. "Well, I suggest you call PJ and get him to pick you up. I'm going to bed."

She strode into her house and was about to slam the door in his face but stopped when he blurted, "I still love you."

Holly turned around and raked her gaze over him. Standing there in the dim light from her porch lamp, she couldn't deny that he looked like hell. It wasn't his physical appearance so much. No, it was the mental anguish on his handsome face. "Dammit," she muttered. Shaking her head, unable to believe what she was about to do, she jerked her head. "Come in. We can talk while you wait for your ride."

Ryan let out a sigh of relief and stepped into the house. He was careful to leave his boots by the door, something he'd always done while they'd been dating. Then he pulled out his phone and sent a text. He glanced up at Holly. "Do you mind if we sit on the couch?"

"Fine. But I'm going to make some decaf first. I need something to warm me up." She took off for the kitchen, mildly annoyed when she heard his light footsteps behind her. She'd been planning on taking a moment to collect herself before she had to deal with him. Instead, she ignored him and went about her business brewing the coffee.

"I need to apologize," Ryan said.

"Okay." Holly pulled the milk out of the fridge and reached for the sugar jar in her spice cabinet. "For what exactly? Showing up here when I was clearly on a date or bailing on me two years ago?"

"Both." He took the sugar and put a teaspoon-full in each of the mugs, proving that he remembered how she liked her coffee.

"Fine. You're forgiven. Is that all you wanted?" She had her arms crossed over her chest and she knew she sounded hostile.

But dammit, it was close to midnight, and Ryan wasn't the man she wanted in her house.

"No... There's something else I need to say." He swallowed hard and glanced away.

The coffee pot made a loud gurgling noise, alerting her to the fact that the coffee was done. She filled both mugs then put a splash of milk in his and a more generous amount in her own. "Here." She handed him his cup. "Now we can go back into the living room."

Without waiting for him to respond, she took off for her couch, kicked off her high heels, and curled up in the corner, tucking her legs beneath her dress. If Ryan hadn't been there, she'd have run upstairs to change before enjoying her coffee, but she wasn't going to talk with Ryan while in her pajamas. She'd just have to wait him out.

His phone pinged with a text. After he read it, he groaned and then showed it to Holly.

Sorry man. The snow is too heavy already on this side of town. I think you're stranded.

Holly wanted to scream. But she held it in and got up to peer out of the window. Sure enough, the snow was piling up quickly. She thought of Amelia and Rex and wondered if they'd gotten back to his cabin. Probably not. Rex said he'd come by after the appointment. She fished out her own phone and tapped out a text to Rex. *Heard the roads are closing. Are you stuck at the healer's office?*

His reply was almost instantaneous. *Yes. We just found out. Looks like the healer wants Amelia to stay here anyway. See you in the morning?*

I'll have coffee on. After Holly hit Send, she put her phone on the coffee table and resumed her position on the sofa.

"Okay. I'm ready. Lay it on me," she said, ready for him to

stop dragging this out. "Whatever you came all the way to Christmas Grove to tell me, I'm all ears."

Ryan slipped his hand into his pocket and pulled out a very shiny, very familiar diamond ring. "Remember when I said that when I got married I wanted my wife to have my mother's ring?"

She raised one eyebrow. "Yes. So?"

He turned to face her. "I know your answer is going to be no. I've seen the way you look at Rex. But I also know he isn't staying in town. You deserve to have someone here to take care of you. You've been alone for far too long, Holly."

She stared at the ring. Then she stared at Ryan and wanted to punch him in the nose. "I don't need anyone to take care of me," she said carefully. "And I'm not alone, either. I have Ilsa. And Zach. And everyone at the library. Not to mention the—" She abruptly stopped talking, hating that she felt like she was justifying her life to him. "I'm not lonely. So don't come in here and act like you're saving me from something."

"I… dammit!" He ran a frustrated hand through his perfect hair. "That's not what I meant at all. Of course you can take care of yourself. You've been doing it for years. And you have more friends than anyone I know. I just meant that I wanted to be the one who gets to take care of you."

"Oh." That was a hell of a lot better speech. Still, Ryan wasn't the one she wanted to take care of her. The problem was she knew the one she wanted wasn't available for the role. She took a good long look at Ryan then. He was still handsome in his pretty-boy way. And he appeared as sincere as ever. But his timing sucked, and she realized that while she'd loved him back then, she hadn't loved him the way that she loved Rex. And even if she couldn't have Rex, she wanted that kind of love in her life. "Listen—"

"Before you say anything, I have to get the rest of this out." Ryan slid off the couch and kneeled down on one knee.

"Ryan. This isn't—"

"Holly," he said, cutting her off. "I already know the answer, but I have to do this. Please."

There was a determination in his tone that had her sitting back and waiting him out. "All right."

He held the ring with two fingers as he stared into her eyes. "I loved you when I left Christmas Grove. My leaving didn't have anything to do with the way I felt about you. I just needed to be on my own, to make it outside of this town before I committed to anyone. I was too restless, Holly."

She nodded because she knew those things to be true.

"I really did intend to return and propose. I bought the ticket. I had the suit. But when it came time to get on the plane, I knew I wasn't ready. It was a real chickenshit move to send you that card. I was a coward. I should have come home and been honest with you. The problem was that I knew if I did that, I'd stay and end up giving up the career I worked so hard for."

"So you didn't. I get it. You had to put your own dreams first. That's not necessarily a bad thing, Ryan."

He choked out a humorless laugh. "Fancy finance jobs don't keep you warm at night, Holly."

She shrugged. "I imagine they don't. Is that what changed your mind and brought you back? You wanted me to keep your bed warm?" It was a mean thing to say, but she couldn't help herself. He'd wounded her so deeply when he'd stepped out of her life, it was hard to maintain the high ground.

"No." He peered at her, his eyes narrowed. "You knew that wasn't true, didn't you?"

She shrugged one shoulder. "If you just needed someone to

warm your bed, I'm sure you wouldn't have any shortage of volunteers."

He glanced away, his face flushing a light shade of pink. "That's what I thought."

"I never cheated on you," he insisted.

"I didn't say you did," she countered. "But I never imagined you were celibate after you called it off either."

He blew out a breath and picked at an imaginary piece of lint on his jeans. "That's not what I'm here to talk about."

She wanted to laugh but swallowed the urge. "Fine. Then talk."

"I was laid off a few months ago. It was nothing to do with performance. Just a restructuring. Our entire department was axed. Anyway, it made me take a hard look at what I wanted out of this life. What it came down to was that I kept seeing myself here with you while doing some financial planning on the side. Every time I closed my eyes, that's the image I saw. Me working to help couples save for their futures while you paint up in your sanctuary. Then we'd have date nights at Noelle's and day hikes up in the mountains. It all just seemed like a perfect dream, and I can't believe I threw that all away."

"It does seem like a perfect dream. But you know real life doesn't work that way," she said.

"It could if we wanted it to," he said and then pressed the ring into her palm. "Holly Reineer, I've loved you ever since the first time I saw you. I know I've made mistakes. Lots of them. But through it all, I never stopped loving you. I'd very much like it if you'd give me a chance to prove to you that I will never take you for granted again. Decisions made about our future will be for the good of both of us. I want us to be a family. Will you consider taking me back and letting me earn the right to call you my wife one day?"

Holly stared so hard at that ring that her eyes started to water. Or was she just crying? She didn't know. He'd given her one hell of a speech. Sure, he'd fumbled it in places, but he'd finished strong. Her answer to a proposal was a solid no. But he'd just asked her to consider taking him back. Considering wasn't committing. Did she owe him that? Probably not. She didn't owe anyone anything. But she did find herself wanting to think things through before she closed the door on him forever. Did it matter if her love for him was more muted than her love for Rex? Her heart screamed *yes*, but her head insisted that the fire fades and the key to a good marriage is to marry your best friend. He had been her best friend once.

She wiped at her eyes. It was late, and all the thoughts of reconnecting with Ryan were jumbling around in her head. She stood, closed her hand around the ring and said, "I'll think about it."

She made it halfway up the stairs when Ryan called, "Hols?"

"Yeah?"

"Can I sleep on your couch?"

She nodded. "Sure. The linens are still in the hall closet."

CHAPTER 27

*R*ex was dead on his feet as he trudged through the snow to Holly's house. He'd barely slept a wink the night before while watching over Amelia at the Healer's office. Thankfully, Amelia was fine and so was the baby. The healer had sent them home with some prenatal energy potions, strict orders to lose the cinchers until after the baby was born, and to eat five small meals a day to keep her blood sugar levels normal.

After getting the all clear from the healer that it was safe for Amelia to head home, Rex was grateful for his truck and the snow tires he'd put on the week before. They'd been able to make it through the snow-filled streets without having to wait for anyone to plow.

Rex didn't waste any time when Amelia jumped in the shower. He left his sister a note and took off for Holly's house. He was dying to see his girl, to wrap his arms around her. He imagined her sitting at her table, sipping a cup of coffee, and nibbling on a cookie because he wasn't there to cook for her.

He smiled when the back of her house came into view. And

when he climbed the stairs of the back porch, he caught movement in the window but couldn't see anything more than an outline due to the window shade being closed. But she was in there, and that was all that mattered.

It wasn't a surprise that the back door was unlocked. It almost always was. But it was a surprise to find Ryan, Holly's ex, standing in her kitchen in his boxer shorts, drinking out of Rex's favorite mug. "What the hell are you doing here?" he growled at the man.

Ryan turned and eyed Rex as he lowered the mug to the counter. "I stayed over. What are you doing here?"

"I came to see Holly." Rex was frozen in the doorway as he took in the scene. The man was in his boxers for god's sake. Ryan had stayed over. What exactly had gone on the night before?

"She's in the shower," he said. "Is it important? I could let her know you're here."

There was a smugness about the bastard that Rex wanted to knock right out of the man. "It's not important," he forced out. The idea of Ryan heading into Holly's bathroom while she was naked in the shower was enough to make Rex's stomach roll. But who was he kidding? Ryan was roaming around her kitchen in his boxers. Was there any question that he'd already gotten a peek at the goods the night before? Rex had a hard time reconciling that thought. Holly was the loyal type. She wouldn't cheat on him, would she?

But would it even be cheating? Rex was leaving soon. Maybe she and Ryan had patched things up after all. As much as he hated everything about the guy standing in front of him, he knew that had everything to do with the way he felt about Holly, and not much to do with the man himself. Suddenly he needed to get out of there. He needed to breathe, think, maybe punch something. "Tell Holly I came by and that Amelia is home and doing fine. Can you do that for me?"

Ryan jerked back slightly as if he were surprised that Rex was leaving. Then his face went completely blank as he said, "Sure, man. I'll be sure to do that."

Rex gave him a quick nod and then disappeared back out the door.

～

"THAT WAS FAST," Amelia said when Rex walked through the front door of his cabin. "I figured you'd want a quickie this morning, but that was fast even for you," she teased.

Rex let out a low growl and headed for the coffee pot. "Is this decaf?"

"No," she said, eyeing him with concern. "What happened at Holly's?"

"She got back together with her ex. I don't want to talk about it." He poured himself the largest cup of coffee ever known to man and then stomped off into his bedroom, leaving Amelia gaping after him.

Three hours later, Rex emerged and sat on the sofa next to Amelia. "I've been checking the weather for the next week, and I think it's best if we leave for Keating Hollow tomorrow morning."

"That's before the toy drive exchange," she said gently.

"I know." He grimaced. "I hate to miss that, but we need to get you to Keating Hollow, preferably before Christmas so you have a few days to settle in before you start your new job. And if it snows too much, it will be hard to get over the pass. Holly will take care of the toy drive. I'm sure Zach and Ilsa will help her out. Everything's sorted, wrapped, and ready to go anyway. All they need to do is act as Santa's elves."

"And Evan? What about his gift?" she prodded.

There was no denying that Rex wanted to be there to see the joy and excitement on the little guy's face when he dug into all the baking supplies he and Holly had picked out for him, but the desire to leave Christmas Grove was too strong. He couldn't handle seeing Holly and Ryan together. He just couldn't. He already felt as if his heart had been ripped out of his chest. Just like it had been when he'd walked in on Sara and her lover all those years ago. Only this time it was worse because now he knew that Holly Reineer was the love of his life and they'd never be together.

There must have been something in his eyes that convinced Amelia to not ask any more questions because she placed a soft hand on his knee and said, "Okay, big brother. We can leave tomorrow."

He nodded, and without another word he disappeared into the bedroom to pack up his meager belongings.

CHAPTER 28

$\mathcal{H}$olly checked her phone for what seemed like the thousandth time. Rex hadn't shown up, and he hadn't answered her text. But she knew from Amelia's text that they were back at his cabin. She hadn't wanted to grill Amelia about why Rex had gone radio silent, so she'd left it alone and spent her day off baking. It was what she did when she was anxious. By the time the afternoon rolled around, she had over six dozen cookies baked and ready to be decorated.

A soft knock on the back door startled her. Who the heck was that? If it was Rex, surely he'd just let himself in, wouldn't he?

She moved to the door and pulled it open, finding Rex standing there with one hand holding the back of his head as he stared at the porch. "Hey," she said. "What's wrong?"

He lifted his head and the expression there nearly tore Holly's heart out.

"You look like someone stole your puppy. Get in here so I can stuff you full of cookies and find out what's bothering you. Is it Amelia? Is she all right?"

"Amelia's fine," he said, his voice gruff, but he didn't move from his spot on the porch. "I just came by to let you know that Amelia and I need to leave early for Keating Hollow. There's weather in the forecast so we're going to take off in the morning. Early."

Holly's stomach dropped straight to her toes. She'd known his plans had changed and they were leaving soon after Christmas instead of New Year's, but she'd thought they had a few more days. She hadn't even finished his gift yet. "That's... um, yeah. I guess if you need to leave because of the weather, then that's what you need to do."

"Right." Rex's gaze bore into her, and she had the feeling that he was searching for something, but she didn't know what.

"Do you want to come in?" she tried again.

Rex shook his head. "I don't think that's a good idea. It's probably better for both of us if we just make a clean break. It'll be less messy that way."

She blinked at him, willing herself to not cry. She didn't want him to see her a blubbering mess. "You're probably right about that. Does this mean you'll be going straight to New York from Keating Hollow?"

He averted his eyes and gazed out at the snowy yard. "Yeah."

"I see." Because coming back to Christmas Grove to see her one last time wouldn't be a clean break. "All right then. I guess this is it."

"I guess so." Rex continued to stand there as if he were made of stone. Perhaps he was hoping his heart would turn to marble so that he wouldn't have to deal with any emotions surrounding their separation. Holly knew he cared for her. It had been obvious right up until this very minute.

"Dammit, Rex," she said, unable to control her frustration as she walked out onto her porch barefoot. "Kiss me goodbye and tell me how much this meant to you."

His blue eyes flashed with pain just before he crushed his lips to hers and kissed her with everything he had. His arms came around her, holding her tightly to his body as his tongue lashed against hers, all violent and loving and needy. His kiss was telling her everything he couldn't say. He wanted her, didn't want to leave, couldn't stay, felt more than he was willing to admit to even himself. It all came out in the kiss, and when they finally pulled apart, they were both breathing hard.

"I'm going to miss you, Hols," he said quietly.

"Me, too," she said, her voice trembling with emotion.

"I had a really good time with you this month, and for the record, I really don't think that love potion had anything to do with it."

Despite the fact that her heart was shattering into a million pieces, she chuckled and said, "You're right. It didn't. I overreacted just a bit that day at the tree-lighting."

"Maybe a little." He gave her the tiniest of smiles then cupped her chin, raising it just a little so that he could make eye contact. "You deserve better than Ryan."

She jerked back a little purely from surprise. "I know that."

"Are you sure?" His eyes narrowed, and as his mouth curved down into a frown, she could feel disapproval rolling off him.

"I'm sure. What's this about?" she demanded.

"Holly..." He sucked in a deep breath and blew it out. "Never mind. I just want what's best for you, gorgeous. And I know it isn't him."

Holly let out a low chuckle. "You know. That's exactly what I told him last night."

Rex blinked. "You did?"

"Yep. He showed up here, still trying to get me back. He proposed and everything."

"You're making it sound like you said no," Rex said, confusion rolling over his features again.

"Of course I did. Or at least I did this morning when I kicked him out." She grinned at him. "He asked me to consider it, and I was too tired to argue the point so I told him I would. But this morning, all I could think about was the fact that I wanted you in my bed. And I just knew that there was no going back there with Ryan. I know you're leaving, but I deserve to have someone I'm excited about. Not someone safe." She pressed her palm to his chest and gazed up at him. "It was awfully lonely without you last night."

He let out a choked laugh. "Three's a crowd don't you think?"

She frowned, trying to figure out what he meant. "Um, it was only me in my bed. Who is this mythical third person?"

"Ryan stayed the night, Holly. I'm not an idiot. No man makes a woman coffee in his boxers if he didn't spend the night with her."

Holly just stared, open-mouthed. "You think I slept with Ryan?"

"Didn't you?"

Holly threw her head back and laughed. She laughed so hard her eyes actually started to water. When she finally came up for air, she said, "No. He slept on the couch. He didn't even make me coffee. The selfish bastard used the last of my grounds and then told me I could drink tea. That was when I threw him out on his ass. The only reason he stayed was because of the snow."

"Oh." Rex shook his head. "What a complete ass. I bet he didn't tell you I came by this morning, either, did he?"

"You did?"

He nodded. "You were in the shower."

"Is that why you ghosted me most of the day? You thought I slept with Ryan?" Her voice had risen a couple of octaves, and her incredulity was off the charts.

"I might have reacted badly. It was a shock to see him here, and then I started getting flashbacks of Sara and I..." He shrugged. "I'm sorry. It wasn't my finest hour."

Holly's entire body went numb as she realized what Rex must've relived when he thought another woman he cared about had cheated on him. Her heart ached just thinking about it. She slipped her hand into his and gently pulled him into her kitchen. "You listen to me, Rex Holiday. You do not need to apologize to me for how that made you feel. I get it. I really do. You should know that I'm the faithful sort. I don't cheat, and I'd never do that to you in a million years. Do you understand what I'm saying?"

"Yeah." He smiled down at her. "I get it."

"Good. Now are you going to stay here a while? There are some things I'd like to show you in the bedroom."

"Yes. I am. But you do realize we only have about sixteen more hours before I leave town. Maybe we should get started on the make-up sex now so we have time for goodbye sex, good morning sex, and after dinner sex. What do you say?"

"I'm going to need to add in shower sex, after dessert sex, and maybe afternoon sex, too."

"We should order in. We're going to need our strength," he said as he walked her backward toward the stairs.

"There's no time for that," she said, tugging on his shirt and pulling it over his head. "If we get weak, there's frozen pizza in the freezer."

"You did not just say that," Rex murmured as he nuzzled her neck. "I don't do prepackaged frozen food."

"Looks like it's cookies for dinner then," she said as she turned and ran up the stairs.

"Works for me," he said when he strode into her room and slammed the door behind him.

CHAPTER 29

"*I* don't think I can stay in this town," Ilsa said as she stared out the window of the Enchanted Bean Stalk. It was the day of the town holiday gift exchange, and instead of Zach and Ilsa helping her sort and pass out the packages, it was just going to be Ilsa. Zach had apparently escaped to Keating Hollow after his and Ilsa's big night together. He'd sent Holly a text but had gone radio silent on Ilsa. And neither of them knew when he was coming back.

"Why? Because Zach bailed on you? What about me? I need you here," Holly said, trying not to think about the other man who was in Keating Hollow at the moment. After their last day and night together, they'd talked about keeping in touch, but ultimately, Holly had been the one to put the brakes on that idea. It would just be too hard to move on if they were texting and talking all the time. So they'd said a tearful goodbye and had cut off contact cold turkey.

It sucked. Hard.

"Yes, because Zach bailed on me. We had a great time together. Fantastic, really, and now look what happened. I feel like the town bicycle." She buried her face in her hands and shook her head.

"Please, Ilsa. I know you're upset, but aren't you being a little dramatic? You're hardly the town bicycle. Hardly anyone has taken you for a ride. Besides, that expression is really awful and shaming toward women. I'm banning you from using it again."

Ilsa wiped at her eyes. "You're right. It is awful. I just meant that I feel used. I thought Zach and I had something special going, but the minute he got me out the door, he bolted."

"Wait, Rex and Amelia didn't leave until two days after the ball. Just how long were you at Zach's house?"

Her face turned quite a bright color of red. "Three days."

"Whoa. That's... impressive." Holly stared at her friend in wonder. "I hope you stayed hydrated."

Ilsa laughed. "We did." Then she sobered. "I thought we were on the same page. He definitely wasn't hinting for me to leave. In fact, I was intending to go home the day after the ball, but he was the one who tugged his shirt off me and tossed me back on his bed. We—"

"That's enough," Holly said, holding up a hand. "I don't need any details."

"Right." Ilsa studied her coffee mug. "I just don't get it. And I'm tired of being jerked around. Zach can switch from hot to cold in a nanosecond. I have no idea what the issue is, but I don't think I can handle it anymore. Did I tell you my cousin offered me a management job at her party store just outside of Sacramento? Apparently the last manager made a huge mess of everything, and she needs someone she trusts to come in and clean it up."

"She did? Does it pay well?"

Ilsa nodded. "And she offered me her guest house, so I can stay there rent free while I get her store in shape.

"That actually sounds like a good deal. Would you give up your place here?" Holly just kept asking questions in an effort to not freak out. First Rex had left and now Ilsa looked like she'd be next. Only they'd still see each other. Sacramento was only a few hours away.

"Yeah, I think so. I'm on a month-to-month lease now, so it's no big deal." She took another sip of her coffee. "If I come running back to Christmas Grove, can I stay with you until I find my own place?"

"What? Of course." Holly gave her friend a stern look. "You know my door has always been open to you. In fact, I think you should give up your apartment, quit your job here, and move in with me while you start your own party planning business. Forget working for anyone else."

"That sounds really wonderful, Holly," Ilsa said. Her voice was low, and Holly could tell her friend was on the verge of crying. Normally Holly would try to comfort her, but now wasn't the time. Ilsa didn't want to break down in public and certainly not right before the gift exchange. "But," Ilsa continued, "I think I need a change of scenery for a while, and helping my cousin is something I'll feel good about."

"It sounds like you already have your mind made up," Holly said.

She nodded. "I think so. I'll leave right after Christmas."

"I'll miss you," Holly said.

"You'll come visit me for New Year's and we'll have an epic pajama party with ice cream, Krispy Creams, and champagne. What do you say?"

It was the New Year's they dreamed of as kids. Holly chuckled. "It sounds perfect."

Late that afternoon, the gift exchange went off without a hitch. Kids squealed in excitement over their gifts, while parents hid tears of joy. Holly had found herself trapped in more than two dozen hugs before the event was over. But by far, her most favorite part of the afternoon was when Evan had opened up a present to find a smaller version of his stuffed wolf that he'd donated, along with a note that said he was one of Benji's puppies and that Benji wanted Evan to raise him.

Evan had hugged the wolf so tightly, Holly was afraid it's head might pop right off. But it was so touching that she and Lily had to dry each other's tears. There was no doubt that Rex had been the architect of that gift. And Holly couldn't have loved him more for it.

She'd held back the baking supplies until after everyone else had left. She'd asked Lily to stay a little longer, and once it was just them and Ilsa, she'd sat them down and presented the gifts. "I know it looks like a lot, but a secret Santa saw just how dedicated Evan is to his baking classes and wanted to make sure he could practice his techniques any time he wants." She smiled at Evan and Lily. "These gifts are for both of you."

The pair spent the next five minutes tearing through the gift paper, gasping, crying, and high-fiving each other. It was the most beautiful mother-son exchange that Holly had ever witnessed. She'd spent the entire time taking picture after picture with the intent to share them with Rex, even though they were supposed to quit each other cold turkey. He deserved to see the happiness he'd brought to Lily and Evan and the whole town of Christmas Grove.

After fielding a hundred thank yous from Lily and giving them both more hugs than she could count, finally Ilsa and Holly were left to clean up the remnants of Christmas.

"It's almost sad, isn't it?" Ilsa said, sounding maudlin.

"What's sad?" Holly asked, tying off a large garbage bag full of wrapping paper.

"The moments right after you open presents. All of the excitement had dissipated, the floor is a mess, and then you're left with the knowledge that you still have to clean up. There's nothing left to look forward to other than maybe some left over Christmas cookies. It's like a little death, that's all."

"Okay. That's enough," Holly said to Ilsa. "It's time for us to go get dinner and then have a Christmas movie marathon. You still like those, right?"

Ilsa shrugged. "I guess."

"Don't sound too excited. I might get a fat head knowing how much you love hanging out with me," Holly joked.

Ilsa gave her a half-hearted smile as she followed her out of the building.

~

IT WAS LATE when Holly finally got around to texting Rex the pictures she'd taken of Evan and Lily. Ilsa had fallen asleep in her bed during the last Christmas flick. Holly wasn't tired, so she slipped out and made her way downstairs to the sofa, where she spent way too much time weeding through the pictures to send Rex. All but two she sent to Rex showed Evan's smiling face. One was of Lily wiping her eyes, and the last one was the back of Evan as he hung on tight to Lily in a massive hug. Lily's eyes were closed, but despite that, there was so much love and joy in her expression it was hard to miss.

The only words Holly texted to Rex were, *Miss you. Wish you were here.*

Her fingers were itching to type that she loved him, but she didn't go through with it. That would only make things harder.

It wasn't long after Holly sent the text that she dozed off on the couch and woke up to a series of pings on her phone.

She quickly tapped the screen and felt her heart melt when she saw that Rex had answered her.

That kid deserves the world. I'm glad you were there. I'm sorry I missed it. Tell them Merry Christmas from me.

Then there were a bunch of pictures of a cute cottage with the caption, *Amelia's house,* followed by, *I miss you, too.*

Pure joy soared through her heart as she read those four tiny words. She knew it was silly. Of course he'd tell her he missed her. She had no doubt that he did. They'd become close over the last month. Even so, it wasn't as if he'd confessed his undying love to her. He'd only mentioned that he missed her.

Smiling to herself, she started to scroll through the pictures. The place was very cute with a tidy kitchen, large living room, pretty yard that backed up to the redwoods and two bedrooms. The master was large with a decent sized spa-tub in the bathroom. And the second bedroom—Holly studied it and gasped out loud. It was already furnished for a nursery. For Amelia's baby. She was pregnant after all. But it was the details that caught her eyes. The crib, the pale blue wall color, the sunflower stencils on the wall. The baby that had been in her vision belonged to Amelia, not Rex.

Relief rushed through her, leaving her lightheaded. And without thinking too hard about it, she pressed Rex's number and called him.

"Hols?" he said into the phone.

"I'm in love with you," she blurted. "I don't care if you travel. I'll make it work. I'll get therapy if I have to. I'll move to New York or travel with you. Or whatever you want. I don't want this to end. Not now, not ever. If you feel the same way, let me know, because I'm willing to do what it takes to be with you."

There was silence on the other end of the line.

Holly's gut turned, and she felt like she might vomit. "Rex?"

"I'm here," he said softly.

There was more silence over the line. Finally, when Holly couldn't take it anymore, she said, "Obviously you don't feel the same way. Forget I said anything. It's late. I'm probably not thinking straight. Don't worry about this. It's fine. I'll talk to you later. Or not. Or... I don't know. Just, Merry Christmas to you and Amelia."

"Merry Christmas to you, too, Holly," he said.

Tears stung her eyes as she said, "Thanks," and then ended the call.

CHAPTER 30

$\mathcal{H}$olly woke the next morning to pounding on her front door. She sat up with a start and then rolled off the couch, causing her to hit her head on the coffee table. "Ouch. Son of a…"

"Holly?" a familiar male voice called from the other side of the door.

"Rex?" She scrambled to her feet and hurried to the door, quickly unlocking it to find the man of her dreams standing there with two suitcases beside him.

Without a word, he stepped inside her house and pulled her into his arms, hugging her and burying his face in her hair.

Unable to believe he was really there, she wrapped her arms around him and ran her hands up and down his back just for confirmation that he was actually real and not a figment of her imagination or some sort of cruel dream. "Are you really here?"

"I'm not just here, I'm back… for good." He pulled away, putting a little distance between them. "I'm sorry, Holly. I should've told you exactly how I felt the minute you told me you love me. I can't imagine how that phone call made you feel."

"Um, like an idiot," she supplied, feeling the tears form again just by thinking about it.

Rex brought one hand up and brushed a tear away. "I'm in love with you, too."

"You are?" she asked, even though she knew deep down in her gut that he was. There was no question about it.

"I'm sure. And while I can't promise I won't ever leave on trips for work, I do promise I'll always come back to you wherever you are. Here, New York, some other place that we decide we want to live. But if I have a choice, I'd prefer here in Christmas Grove in this gorgeous house. What do you say?"

She was completely speechless as she got lost in his gorgeous blue eyes.

"Holly?" he said with a chuckle. "Did you hear me?"

"She heard you," Ilsa said from the top of the stairs. "She's just trying to process it all."

Ilsa glided down the stairs dressed in jeans and a white sweater. "Holly, give the man an answer before he blows a blood vessel in his brain."

Holly grinned at Ilsa and then turned her attention back to her man. "Yes, we can live here. But my offer still stands. If we need to move around a bit, I'm okay with it. As long as we're together."

Rex let out a sigh of relief and then pulled her back into a desperate hug.

"Good. I'm glad you two got that worked out. Now I'm off to celebrate Christmas Eve with my parents. Hols, you and Rex are welcome if you want. If you have... ahem... other plans, don't feel obligated."

Holly giggled into Rex's neck. "I'll text you and let you know how the day shapes up."

Ilsa snickered. "Make sure you don't leave out any of the juicy details." The door clicked shut, leaving Rex and Holly alone in the big Victorian.

"I can't believe you're here," Holly said, running her hands all over him. "What made you drop everything and come here today?"

"Isn't it obvious?"

She shook her head.

"You laid it all on the line for me. You said you're in love with me." He cupped her cheek with his big rough hand. "I'm in love with you, too Holly Reineer, and you're my person. I'm all in. There's no other witch I'd rather be with on Christmas than you."

The tears fell unchecked down her cheeks as she stared at the man she loved. "You're... I'm..." She squeezed her eyes shut and reopened them as if to make sure she wasn't seeing things. "I love you, Rex."

"I love you, too, Holly."

She grinned and slipped her hand into his. "There's something I wanted to give you for Christmas, but I didn't get a chance before you left."

As she tugged him up the stairs, he chuckled. "I think you gave me plenty before I left."

"Don't be a perv. I'm not taking you to my bedroom."

Although, as it turned out, she did make a pitstop in her bathroom to brush her teeth and tame her couch hair. But as soon as she was done, she continued to the third floor, into her artist's loft. "I never got a chance to show you what I do in my down time."

Rex glanced around at the paintings. There were a lot more than were there the day he'd stumbled into the room.

"I've been painting a lot since you left," she said.

"I can see that," he replied.

Her eyebrows shot up. "You've been in here before?"

"Just once. It was the day I was looking for Sabrina."

She smirked at him. "But you never asked me about my paintings."

He shrugged. "I figured you say something when you were ready."

"You're a smart man... sometimes," she said as she pulled him over into the corner and turned her latest piece so that he could see it. "I made this for you."

He let out a small gasp and grabbed her hand again, squeezing it as he stared at the painting of him and his sister with their heads bent together as they laughed about something one of them had said.

"It's fantastic," Rex said. "I mean, you've captured us completely and painted something magical, Hols."

She felt herself flush with his praise. "Thank you. I felt a lot of joy as I painted it."

"That definitely shines through," he said and gave her a soft kiss on the top of her head. He stared at it for a minute longer and then said, "My turn. Come on. Your gifts are downstairs."

"Gifts?" she asked.

He just smiled and guided her back to the living room. After pulling his luggage in from the porch, he dug in one of his suitcases and pulled out a picture frame. "This is what I do in my spare time."

She turned the frame over and spotted a black and white photo of her and Evan in their baking class. They were laughing, and both she and Evan had sparkling eyes. She lifted her gaze to his. "How did you take this without us knowing?"

He shoved his hands into his jean pockets and gave her a self-satisfied smile. "I use my smart phone. Sometimes I get lucky and the shot is perfect. This is one of those."

"It's wonderful, Rex. I love it." She threw her arms around him and kissed him. They stood there, kissing and whispering for a long time before Holly pulled away and said, "I thought there were *gifts*. As in more than one."

"Right. Go get the one under your tree," he said.

"I knew it was from you," she said as she hurried over and retrieved the mystery present she'd received earlier in the month.

"Go on. Open it."

She did as she was told, and inside the plain white box she found a journal that had *Love Spells* scrawled across the leather cover. She looked up at him and laughed. "This is the perfect gift."

"Open it to the first page. I wrote you a little something."

Eager to find out what he wrote, she opened the book to the first page and found a poem.

Roses are red
Violets are blue
I used to think potions and spells were only for fools
But that's all changed because a love spell brought me to you

"That's really cheesy," Holly teased, loving him even more than she ever thought possible.

"You think it's brilliant," he countered.

"You might be right," she said and then dropped the journal

on the coffee table. "Now, let's go upstairs and make some Christmas magic."

"If you insist. Got any love potions up there?" he asked with a smirk.

She gave him a seductive smile. "Yep. Which one do you want to try first?"

His eyes turned a molten shade of blue-silver as he said, "All of them."

CHAPTER 31

ELEVEN MONTHS LATER

For the first time in eleven months, Ilsa McKenzie drove back into her hometown of Christmas Grove. Her palms sweated against the steering wheel despite the fact it was roughly thirty degrees outside. She'd turned the heat up to keep it toasty in the used Ford Escape she'd purchased four months ago. But even if she hadn't, she was pretty sure her palms would still be sweating.

There was someone she'd come home to see, and she was dreading it.

Zach Frost.

He was the one man she'd always loved and the one man who'd ripped her heart out after the best three days of her life. She'd left shortly after that and had been managing her cousin's party supply store near Sacramento ever since. But it was time to come home to the foothills of Christmas Grove. Mistakes had been made, and she was ready to face them.

An ache had formed in her stomach when she thought about Zach.

She pushed the thoughts of her old flame out of her mind

and steered the car toward the edge of town and down the street that led to Holly and Rex's place. She bit down on her bottom lip. Rex was Zach's best friend.

Crap. There she was, thinking about Zach again.

Maybe he was too busy with his Christmas tree farm to be milling around Holly's place. One could only hope. With a prayer and a few wishes for good luck, she turned in to the long drive that led up to Holly's house. People were milling around the old pumpkin patch, erecting a giant tent. She smiled as she realized they were once again putting up a Christmas scene of the Great Hall from the Harry Potter books so that the kids in town could be sorted into houses and residents could drop off toys for the town toy drive. Rex and Holly had dreamed up the decorative theme the year before, and it looked like they were all in this year with a few added touches. The ghosts from Hogwarts were hanging from a tree branch, while a house elf sat at the base of the tree. It was likely that Lemon Pepperson, the owner of the delivery service Christmas Grove Express, would animate them for Holly once the tent was in place. She was a powerful air witch and had done a lot of work for them the previous year.

By the time Ilsa pulled up to the front of Holly's old Victorian, she had a huge smile on her face. She really did love Christmas Grove, and despite her nerves she was glad to be home.

"Ilsa!" Holly cried as she ran down her front porch, her arms wide and ready for a hug.

Ilsa quickly hopped out of the small SUV and threw herself into her friend's arms.

"I'm so glad you're finally here," Holly said into her ear. "We've been dying for you and—"

"Ilsa?"

Zach. She'd know that voice anywhere. He had a low rumble that never failed to send a tingle up her spine. It didn't disappoint this time either. She suppressed a shudder and turned around to face him. God, he was gorgeous. Tall, dark hair, even darker eyes that she got lost in so often.

"Hi, Zach," she said with a small wave, ignoring her libido. Now was not the time to lust after the man. "How have you been?"

His gaze swept over her, and she wondered what he saw. Would he notice any changes? Would he care? "Good. Can't complain. We missed having you around, though."

She raised both eyebrows as if to say, *Seriously?*

He averted his gaze and nodded a hello to Rex, who was standing on the front porch watching them. "Hey, man. I came to talk to you about a shipment for up north."

"Yep. Just as soon as we get Ilsa settled, we can go over the orders." The two had become business partners about six months ago after Rex decided he was tired of leaving Holly three or four times a month for his big corporate job that was based out of New York. When he'd up and quit one day, Zach had offered him a partnership in the Christmas tree farm that was next door.

Oh hell. Talk about awkward. She'd put Rex and Holly in a really bad position with her secret, and it was time to rip the bandage off.

"Zach, I—"

"Ilsa," he said at the same time, and they both chuckled.

"You first," Ilsa said, happy to have any excuse to delay telling him her news.

He brushed one hand through his hair. "I need to apologize. What happened after the ball last year... I didn't handle that very well."

Ilsa bit down on her bottom lip, felt herself do it, and immediately let go. She couldn't afford to be vulnerable. Not right then. "Okay. I probably could've handled it better myself," she said, and there was more truth in that statement than he could even comprehend at that moment.

"It was wrong of me to not call you," he said.

"You mean not call me *back*," she said, careful to make the distinction. Because she *had* tried to call him. He'd iced her out for reasons completely unknown to her.

"Right. I should've called you back. I'm sorry. Very sorry." He glanced over at his friend Rex, who was still standing on the porch, and then at Holly, who had the backseat passenger door open as she tried to free the precious cargo. "I was kind of a mess. It wasn't you. I promise."

She had trouble believing that she didn't have anything to do with his disappearance, but honestly, none of that mattered now. There were a lot more important things to discuss.

"Do you think we can get together and—"

The piercing cry of a baby filled the air, followed by Holly plucking the two-month-old child out of the back of Ilsa's car.

"Shh, sweetheart," Holly cooed. "It's okay. Auntie is gonna get you inside where it's warm in just a minute."

Zach glanced over at the baby and then at Ilsa. His lips split into a grin. "You're babysitting?"

Ilsa just stared at him. How dense was he?

When she didn't answer him, Zach tried again, only this time he directed his question at Holly. "What's her name?"

Holly met Ilsa's gaze for just a moment. Ilsa shrugged one shoulder. *Sure, go ahead and tell him*, she said with her body language. He was going to find out sooner or later. Pasting a sweet smile on her face, Holly walked over to Zach. "Zach, meet Mia. Mia meet Zach."

Zach reached out and wrapped a couple of fingers around her hand and gently pumped her arm. "It's nice to meet you, Mia. How do you know Ilsa?"

That was her cue. Ilsa sucked in a deep breath. "I'm her mommy."

"What?" Zach asked, but no one responded. He was looking between Mia and Ilsa, obviously doing some very quick math. "How old is she?"

"Two months," Ilsa said.

His face turned white as everything finally fell into place. "And those phone calls when you said we needed to talk…"

Ilsa didn't say anything for a moment. She took Mia from Holly and then moved closer to Zach. When she was almost brushing her shoulder against his, she turned Mia so that he could gaze down at her, and said, "Zach, I'd like you to meet your daughter, Mia Renee Frost."

DEANNA'S BOOK LIST

Witches of Keating Hollow:
Soul of the Witch
Heart of the Witch
Spirit of the Witch
Dreams of the Witch
Courage of the Witch
Love of the Witch
Power of the Witch
Essence of the Witch

Witches of Christmas Grove:
A Witch For Mr. Holiday
A Witch For Mr. Christmas
A Witch For Mr. Winter

Jade Calhoun Novels:
Haunted on Bourbon Street
Witches of Bourbon Street
Demons of Bourbon Street

Angels of Bourbon Street
Shadows of Bourbon Street
Incubus of Bourbon Street
Bewitched on Bourbon Street
Hexed on Bourbon Street
Dragons of Bourbon Street

Pyper Rayne Novels:
Spirits, Stilettos, and a Silver Bustier
Spirits, Rock Stars, and a Midnight Chocolate Bar
Spirits, Beignets, and a Bayou Biker Gang
Spirits, Diamonds, and a Drive-thru Daiquiri Stand
Spirits, Spells, and Wedding Bells

Ida May Chronicles:
Witched To Death
Witch, Please
Stop Your Witchin'

Crescent City Fae Novels:
Influential Magic
Irresistible Magic
Intoxicating Magic

Last Witch Standing:
Bewitched by Moonlight
Soulless at Sunset
Bloodlust By Midnight
Bitten At Daybreak

Witch Island Brides:
The Wolf's New Year Bride

The Vampire's Last Dance
The Warlock's Enchanted Kiss
The Shifter's First Bite

Destiny Novels:
Defining Destiny
Accepting Fate

Wolves of the Rising Sun:
Jace
Aiden
Luc
Craved
Silas
Darien
Wren

Black Bear Outlaws:
Cyrus
Chase
Cole

Bayou Springs Alien Mail Order Brides:
Zeke
Gunn
Echo

ABOUT THE AUTHOR

New York Times and USA Today bestselling author, Deanna Chase, is a native Californian, transplanted to the slower paced lifestyle of southeastern Louisiana. When she isn't writing, she is often goofing off with her husband in New Orleans or playing with her two shih tzu dogs. For more information and updates on newest releases visit her website at deannachase.com.